HUNTED

OUTRUN. OUTLAST. OUTWIT.

Gripping Tales

Edited By Jenni Harrison

First published in Great Britain in 2020 by:

 Young**Writers**® Est. 1991

Young Writers
Remus House
Coltsfoot Drive
Peterborough
PE2 9BF
Telephone: 01733 890066
Website: www.youngwriters.co.uk

Printed and bound in the UK by BookPrintingUK
Website: www.bookprintinguk.com
YB0436J

FOREWORD

IF YOU'VE BEEN SEARCHING FOR EPIC ADVENTURES, TALES OF SUSPENSE AND IMAGINATIVE WRITING THEN SEARCH NO MORE! YOUR HUNT IS AT AN END WITH THIS ANTHOLOGY OF MINI SAGAS.

We challenged secondary school students to craft a story in just 100 words. In this first installment of our SOS Sagas, their mission was to write on the theme of 'Hunted'. But they weren't restricted to just predator vs prey, oh no. They were encouraged to think beyond their first instincts and explore deeper into the theme.

The result is a variety of styles and genres and, as well as some classic cat and mouse games, inside these pages you'll find characters looking for meaning, people running from their darkest fears or maybe even death itself on the hunt.

Here at Young Writers it's our aim to inspire the next generation and instill in them a love for creative writing, and what better way than to see their work in print? The imagination and skill within these pages are proof that we might just be achieving that aim! Well done to each of these fantastic authors.

So if you're ready to find out if the hunter will become the hunted, read on!

CONTENTS

Shivajith K Pandian (11)	63	Rahan Mankoor (15)	105
Jacob Nuno Levy Parsons (12)	64	Noah Barton (12)	106
Maazin Rizwan (11)	65	Manar El-Kaddu (15)	107
Tasmia Mamun (13)	66	Evie Malcolm-Ward (12)	108
Ella James (11)	67	Eliza Davies (12)	109
Dylan Camilleri (12)	68	Callum Tucker (15)	110
Latrell Wilson (15)	69	Jack Flowers (11)	111
Ella Crockford (12)	70	Dylan Richard Edwards (11)	112
Mia Jean Sturla (12)	71	Jessica Symons (15)	113
Dylan Morgan (15)	72	Ruby Diggins (11)	114
Macey Williams (13)	73	Hana Davies (11)	115
Isabelle Evans-Boon (12)	74	Oliver Selby (12)	116
Nirushni Sudhakar (11)	75	Harley Dudley (11)	117
Sophie Baines (11)	76	Ffion Rankin (11)	118
Ethan Bebb (13)	77	Kiara Thomas (13)	119
Ardit Bullatovci (13)	78	Imogen Hughes (12)	120
Alfie Perriam (12)	79	Macy Watson (13)	121
Issy Wilce (15)	80	Jasmine Lee (11)	122
Seren Carson (16)	81	Lana Hembury (12)	123
Joshua Bryn Nelson-Piney (12)	82	Thalia Lewis-Foran (15)	124
Elle-May Lewis	83	Kacey Paige Jenkins (15)	125
Martin Carter (11)	84	Charlie Drysdale (12)	126
Eva Violet Court (12)	85	Daniel Mackay (12)	127
Ruben James Kelman (12)	86	Amelia Nesbitt-Pearce (14)	128
Phoebe Hopson (11)	87	Henry Parker (12)	129
Oliver Barnett (13)	88	Millie Exintaris (12)	130
Ben Weare	89	Jasmeet Kaur (11)	131
Paris Leaman (11)	90	Joshua Payne (12)	132
Dre Day (15)	91	Harrison James (15)	133
Farah Elise Thomas (12)	92	James Daniel Wilson (12)	134
Max Gardener (11)	93	Evan Heard (11)	135
Naina Luchmun (12)	94	Gabriel Franks (15)	136
Joel Matthew White (12)	95	Daynton Jones (12)	137
Alisha White (14)	96	Abbie Cruse (15)	138
Katie Gardener (12)	97	Mollie Westerman (12)	139
Rhys James Christopher Haines (13)	98	Emma Brotherton (11)	140
		Shannon Lynch (13)	141
Holly Gentle (15)	99	Alfie Sell (12)	142
Sammy Kaur (11)	100	Fabio Correia (11)	143
Charlotte Emily Picton (11)	101	Rhianna Hayes (13)	144
Harvey Herring (11)	102	Dylan John Clarke (13)	145
Nikita Macintosh (12)	103	Will Lewis (14)	146
Elli Roberts	104	Cieran Joshua Williams (12)	147

Ricardo Moreira (12) 148
Lois Taylor (15) 149
Ibrahim Shvan Saadallah (11) 150
Sian Isabel Darnell (11) 151
Millie Tran (11) 152
Mya Gascoyne (13) 153
Owain Andrews (11) 154
Riley Breadmore (12) 155
Daniel Jenkins 156
Molly Mermaid Mary Tina Patsy Kavanagh (12) 157
Jakub Otrusina (13) 158
Maddie McNamee (12) 159
Mason Aaron Cornock (12) 160
Coel Sigerson 161

Malvern St James Girls' School, Great Malvern

Claudia Sefton (11) 162
Panda Lacey (11) 163
Bessy Baxter (12) 164
Phoebe Tabitha Trevelyan (11) 165
Imogen Carys Hayes (12) 166
Amber McAndrew (11) 167
Xuan Xia (11) 168
Evangeline Maya Ede (11) 169
April-Louise Sadler (11) 170
Elizabeth Chloe Motteram (12) 171
Ceri Smith (12) 172
Freya Wall (11) 173
Ilana Coldicott (11) 174
Ella Chan (11) 175
Islay Allen (11) 176
Imogen Hobbs (11) 177
Elizabeth Rose Sylvia Bryant (11) 178
Natalia Rolinson (11) 179
Bethany Williams (12) 180
Madeleine Mary Beckett (12) 181

Rosebery School, Epsom

Mia Getty (11) 182
Holly Hughes-Ehrke (12) 183

Rosie Joyce (13) 184
Mia Cole (12) 185
Eliza Mae Wormley (12) 186
Jas Rae Pelton (12) 187
Eleanor Baldwin (13) 188
Ellah Milner (11) 189

Spalding Grammar School, Spalding

Alexander David Taylor (13) 190
Ryan Ream (13) 191
Isaac Roes (10) 192
Archie Morant (13) 193
Mark Edwards (12) 194
Connor Batch (15) 195
Vedant Gadkari (13) 196
Ben Hales (12) 197
Matthew William Cobb (11) 198
Gregory Pool (11) 199
Thien Clare (12) 200
Caspian Szczygiel (11) 201
Ben Booth (12) 202

St John Rigby College, Orrell

Oskar Leonard (16) 203
Holly Fairhurst (17) 204
Caner Aydin (16) 205
Leah Jeffries (17) 206
Abigail Eve Donlon (17) 207

Stewards Academy, Harlow

Pheobe Dimdore (13) 208
Edward Paul Austin (13) 209
Isabella Constable (11) 210
Taylor Woolley (12) 211
Taygan Harris (12) 212

The Purcell School, Bushey

Thomas Wang (14) 213
Jessica Christine Briany Hendry (14) 214

The Unicorn School, Abingdon

THE STORIES

Venom Of A Hunter

Slaughter. They killed my mother, blood. Dragged my sister with them. They took everything from me... every single thing.

Controlled and devastated my life, but they left one thing, they left behind the purest hatred, malevolence and vengefulness.

All of which emitted from within me. Venom surged through me... I was going to find them, hunt them, destruction, chaos and catastrophe would emerge wherever I went. The power of determination and relentlessness empowered me. So far I had travelled exactly eighty-two kilometres, destroying everything that had confronted me.

I will ruin them! I will destroy them!

I am the hunter.

Ruqayyah Rawat (13)
Barnet Hill Academy, Hendon

My Precious Prey

I saw it... I know I did. Her helpless little legs pushing her faster down the alleyway. What pleasure it was to see her, my dear little victim. My eyes twitching, every essence of fear embraced her lungs to a screeching nightmare. She stopped. Weeping trauma, tears of agony; rapture consumed me. I'm not psychotic. Just the thrill of murder is pleasurable, it's a passion that I must adhere to. Besides, how could I possibly disregard that scrawny pathetic sack of fragile flesh? She was always destined to be my precious corpse. I knew it... I really did.

Asia Aden (12)
Barnet Hill Academy, Hendon

The Halloween Hunter

It's not safe now they know.
It was pitch-black. The rain was crashing down like a hard drum against my window. It was the night before Halloween. The spirits were awake. There was a gleaming full moon gazing down at me. The roads were silent. Suddenly, there was a knock on the door. Frightened to open it. Strangely, a note slid through the door. Hesitant, I finally gained enough courage. It said, 'Beware!' Perplexed, I threw it in the bin, but the thought sauntered in my mind. It was midnight. Someone texted me. That was the last time...

Munira Kone (11)
Barnet Hill Academy, Hendon

The Chase

Boom! Crash! Running for my life, heart pounding out of my chest. All I could see was black as I ran into the darkness ahead of me. I was still holding my blanket, nearly tripping on it, but I wouldn't stop.
I could still hear the voice behind me. I couldn't do it anymore, my legs collapsed. I felt dizzy, the world was spinning around me as I tried to catch my breath. Then I was lying on the ground, in the middle of nowhere. I was terrified. What mess had I got myself into? My life was ruined.

Malayeka Usman (12)
Barnet Hill Academy, Hendon

Danger Approaching?

Calm sea waves greeting my toes. The cold breeze dancing on my skin. The majestic sunset calming my body. I breathed in and out, letting all my stress go down the drain. At least what I thought... All of a sudden the serene sea became enraged. The air laid its harsh breath onto the sea, then on me. I felt a pair of eyes set onto me. I turned around. Nothing to been seen. Nothing. But a reddish-black feather floating in the air gracefully. What was that? Why is it here? I've never seen anything like this before...

Abrish Nadeem (12)
Barnet Hill Academy, Hendon

The Ghostly Birthday

It was 12am and the clock struck on my twelfth birthday, 2020. I was on my iPhone11 and as soon as I looked at the screen, there was a... a... spooky ghost which started to talk to me. All of a sudden, a present appeared from nowhere that I could imagine. It was floating in the air as if a ghost was holding it. I approached the floating present and grabbed it in my shaking hands and all of a sudden, the police arrived. As soon as I opened the present, there was... a werewolf... The chase was on.

Nisa Ahmed (11)
Barnet Hill Academy, Hendon

Corrupted, Imprisoned, Hunted Home

She lived liberally for billions of years, preserving what many called 'home'. A colossus of green-blue exalted in water, air and land. Until she felt a wreck of foreboding. Uncertain that her life would go on for more than a few hundred years. Uncertain of life itself continuing... the once even layer of sea risen to the point where it's diminished half the land. She's a vicious contradiction. People fusing poisons with her. Inflicting on her archaic beauty. Plastic torturing sealife. Animals decaying. People unitedly trying to save their doomed home. But nothing grows without a home. Home is hunted.

Aurora Marrocco (17)
Brighton Hove & Sussex Sixth Form College, Hove

It's Behind You

She couldn't make out further than a few feet in front or behind of her. Her breath was short, her vision blurred, the shots had finally reached her bloodstream. She could barely walk in a straight line. She continued until a feeling of discomfort in her intoxicated stomach arose. She stopped. Silence. Nothing but the sound of her blood roaring. She turned around, her fists clenched. Nothing. She continued to walk, her pulse pounding in her ears, the feeling still hadn't settled. She increased her pace... faster... faster until she was stopped by an unwelcomed hand clasping around her neck...

Scarlett Louise Fox (18)
Brighton Hove & Sussex Sixth Form College, Hove

Aloud

There is noise. Layers of sound reverberating through the surfaces around, so the looted house buzzes with coiled tension. Amongst it all, I remain in my pocket of silence. I fear the wind blowing through the windows. Feel it will carry my scent downwind to them. That they will stalk that trail like a prey's tracks.

The door crashes. Dust falls from their stampede, onto me, below the floorboards. Footsteps slow. The silence is worse than the screams. An audible sniff. My breath strains in my lungs. I'm sure they can hear. There's a crackle of a tannoy. "All clear."

Miriam Akosua Burch Hoefnagels (18)

Brighton Hove & Sussex Sixth Form College, Hove

#Hunted

You're at the computer, in a dimly-lit room. You're tired. This is the sixty-second entry you've read and you'd quite like to tear your eyes out with barbecue tongs. Why do people enter a writing competition when they clearly haven't written so much as a Christmas card before? Imbeciles. You slide your cushioned-but-not-quite-comfy chair back, stand up (pushing down on the table for support, since you're old and getting frail) and walk to the kitchen. The knife rack is half empty, with half of them still in the sink. You take one.
These kids have written their last.

Tom Tresadern (17)
Brighton Hove & Sussex Sixth Form College, Hove

Are You Reading This?

I haven't stopped typing since. I was standing at my window, drawing a heart in the condensation of the glass; he was standing outside, looking up at me. Knowingly. As if he'd found what he had been searching for, tracked me down to this very window. Then he disappeared into the shadows. I haven't stopped typing. I don't know who can help, because I don't really know if I'm in danger. But his eyes told me something was wrong. So know that I won't stop typing, and if I do, something has happened. I won't stop, I need to-

Ruby Davidson (17)
Brighton Hove & Sussex Sixth Form College, Hove

Christmas Havoc

Christmas shopping is like sheep getting herded into an enclosure, rushing to shops, hunting for the perfect gift. Finally, done finding gifts, the problem is there's always one person you forget. "Grandma!" I darted out of the car, dashing into H&M.

"I'm in!"

"Floor three, closing," the speaker belted. My heart pounded. That's the floor where Grandma's gift lay! I crept past the tall bulky guards and charged to the third floor. I sprinted towards the gift, tripped, my bag fell, that's when I noticed I had the gift the whole time... The guards gazed at me. I was hunted.

Sam Locke (13)
Llanishen High School, Llanishen

Them...

We can't run anywhere because there's nowhere left to go. They've had enough. They know we're in danger, they think they're helping us. But they're not; they're the ones endangering us. They're sending us into the cold unwelcoming arms of death when it should be them. We're the worst thing to have happened to this world and we know it. They're trying to encourage a better society, but they're making it worse. They've destroyed everything and nearly everyone. They're fighting for their cause so we will fight for ours, until the very end. I cannot continue now, they are coming...

Hannah Doyle (12)
Llanishen High School, Llanishen

The Party

"Come on Ryan, we've got to get ready for the house party!"
"Okay Dan, I'm ready! Bring the food just in case we get hungry, I've got the car keys."
"Good," said Jack. They arrived at the party and went through the door. It slammed shut behind them. They saw a guy walking towards them, he kicked them out of the door.
"He's holding an axe!" said Ryan. "Run!" Jack started sprinting down the hill, but Ryan fell onto the road, a car driving right next to them.
"Come with me if you want to live!" said the driver. "Quickly!"

Danny Davies
Llanishen High School, Llanishen

Wolf 185

I need to go. They've found us. I could hear someone talking but couldn't make out what he was saying.

"Pups wake up, we need to leave." I was so scared. I ran to the door. "No!" They closed it. I ran to the back towards the boxes. I started to dig. "Almost there," I said to myself. The pups were awake. I heard footsteps. "Hide in the tunnel!" The pups ran towards the tunnel.

"She's in here!" *Bang.* The door slammed open. "Well done, Agent! She has powers and is dangerous..."

Powers, I thought. *I can escape...*

Hollie Rebecca Stevens (13)

Llanishen High School, Llanishen

Hunted

"Hide yourself." That's all I hear when the doors shut right in front of me. I can't believe this! I'm too young to die! "Darren?"

"We need to escape this place Eve," my childhood friend answers me. Again, I hear it again. Is there something wrong with me?

"No, Eve. Don't tell Darren, Eve!" Who is doing this to me? I start to panic. What shouldn't I tell Darren? I crease in confusion. I look at Darren but it's too late. "I'm sorry Eve, you have to understand..." Those are the last words I hear. Locked in there, forever, alone...

Karina Cretu (14)
Llanishen High School, Llanishen

Help!

I still have nightmares about it. It was Friday 13th, the streets were completely deserted, and the weather was bitterly freezing. The sky was wrapped with a blanket of gloominess and the moon glimmered vividly. As I stumbled across the road, the street lights flickered. I could barely see anything.

"Help!" a voice echoed. I instinctively rushed to where the voice came from. My heart pounded rapidly. I did not know what to expect.

"Run for your life!" a voice screeched. I turned around and saw something horrifying that would haunt me for the rest of my life. The nightmares...

Rami Almouseli (13)

Llanishen High School, Llanishen

Seeker

Cold. Harsh. Vile. The creature's breath was causing all the hairs on my body to stand on end like they were trying to come loose and escape this horrid situation. I don't blame them. Wishing I had searched for a better place to hide, I got as low as possible, hoping for a miracle that would turn me invisible, for that was my only hope now. Struggling to keep my nerves under control, praying not to be discovered. "Found you!" Lucy exclaimed, proudly. "You've never been good at this game, have you?"
"No!" I squealed. "The creature has arrived!"

Jackson James Hughes (15)
Llanishen High School, Llanishen

Forbidden Forest

Izzy and Leo entered the forbidden forest. Izzy tripped on a root and shouted, "Go on without me!" Leo scurried on, not knowing what would happen next. Izzy appeared right in front of him. Leo whispered, "How have you not been captured?"

Izzy answered, "I found a place where we could stay!" She led him to a trap and said, "I'm am going to kill you!"

Leo answered, "How could you betray a friend?"

Izzy replied, "I have no friends, you are a mere victim." Izzy drained Leo's life, never to be seen again. Are you next?

Julianna White (12)
Llanishen High School, Llanishen

Hunted

"It's not safe now they know," I panted. "We need to go, now!" My legs were burning and my ears ringing as sirens wailed alarmingly. I paused for a second and glanced at my surroundings. I thought that I was finally free. Deep inside, I knew that they were coming for us, but I couldn't bring myself to move, all the bones in my body ached. The sand was sliding from underneath my feet, making it difficult to run. In the distance, I saw bright blue lights flashing. "Damn it!" I said, fuming. "They found us!"
"Wait, come with me..."

Lilah Drewen (12)
Llanishen High School, Llanishen

Cat And Mouse

The floorboards screamed with the skid of my shoe. The amber headlights pursuing me drew close. Palms sweating, pulse racing. I clumsily swung around corners, the chance of escape seeming impossible. The beast chasing me hissed and clawed at the ground. Fangs snapped at my heels, as I furiously attempted to kick the Devil backwards. I clutched the Holy Grail, shielding it from the monster tailing me. My knees suddenly buckled and my fate was sealed. The demon captured me and greedily snatched the catnip from my grip. It wandered away, merrily purring as I collapsed, breathless and defeated.

Katie Sarah Gill (14)
Llanishen High School, Llanishen

Happy Independence Day

The sirens blazed and the streets were bare. Today could be my death day. Fires roared in the distance and screams were drowned out by the laughter of wicked men. Doors were locked and guns were loaded. It's go time. The rich paid to murder the defenceless and emergency services were granted immunity. But of course, for many of us, protection comes at a high price. It's kill or be killed. "Attention! Happy Independence Day. As of 7pm, until 7am tomorrow, there will be no laws. Take this time to seek revenge and face old enemies, and remember, God bless America."

Sashelle Day (14)
Llanishen High School, Llanishen

Into Nothing

My eyes flickered open, a vermillion haze bled into my vision. Time dilated, my eyes focused, and fire leered, cackling at my macabre fate. Intermittent screaming was hammering within my ribcage. Tears crept between the ash on my face, forming sallow blemishes; my face looked torn apart. Frantically trying to escape, I collapsed. Only then I noticed that the veil of my bones was hanging from my legs - charred, smouldering, reduced to dust. Wallowing in despair, I didn't notice the thump of boots. Despite a gun being raised at my head, I didn't notice. Not until the shot was fired...

Iona Watts (14)
Llanishen High School, Llanishen

Hide-And-Seek (Or Survive)

It started as a game of hide-and-seek but ended as so much more. Sprinting around, he thought there was no chance of being caught in his superb hiding spot but little did he know, he would never emerge. Carefully dashing to his remote hiding place, the roots of the trees grasped at his dirty ankles and his lungs began to burn. Enclosed and encased, breathing was a struggle. *Crunch.* Someone was treading on the crimson leaves. Instantly, the somewhat solid floor dropped. The cannibals often preyed on young victims who were already being hunted... Only his teeth were found.

Sophie Gale (15)
Llanishen High School, Llanishen

The Briefcase

I snatched the briefcase. My legs burned. My bullet wound excruciating. I glanced over to my companion. Struggling to run, it felt like torture. We needed to disappear, but the skyscraper was surrounded. We needed a miracle.
"Look!" shouted my companion. We darted towards the glass elevator. It was risky but we were willing to take the chance. Fortunately, the guards were oblivious. Like a mirage, our escape was waiting loyally. Success! "We got the two billion!" I sighed. All of a sudden my companion held a gun to both of our heads. I didn't think this would happen...

Marcus Cossar (12)
Llanishen High School, Llanishen

The Hunted

The sirens wailed from the rooftops, it was here. Flocks of birds darted from every corner of the city and across the dusky skyline, attempting to escape. Below the street became a panic-fuelled stampede, but I continued spectating. Cowering behind locked doors saved no one. Eventually, it found a way in. Inevitably the slowest of the mass began to fall. A crimson red stream flowed from their mouths as they gasped for air. One by one, the violent spluttering spread throughout the mass until they crumbled to the floor like dominoes. And then silence. It was all going to plan.

Sophie Morris (15)
Llanishen High School, Llanishen

The Chase

"Run!" someone screamed. I spun around and stared into the darkness. I saw the silhouette of a dark creature. I couldn't run for much longer, I wouldn't make it. I collapsed, faceplanting the ground. I was alone. The only light was the torch I was holding. Unwillingly, I shone the torch at it. My screech echoed around me. Its face was covered in scratches, its teeth were pointy and sharp. I screamed again, pain shot through me. Its ears pointed upwards, hair grew from its cheeks. It stood there towering over me. I didn't expect death to feel this way...

Leah Morris (13)
Llanishen High School, Llanishen

Zombiegeddon

"We have to leave. We must find a way out, now!"
Suddenly, there was more banging on the door and I knew
the barricades wouldn't last much longer. We quickly ran up
the creaking stairs and found a secret hatch.
"This is it!" I shouted.
As loud as an explosion, the door smashed open. Like a
cheetah, I opened the hatch and grabbed her arm so we
could climb up. I started climbing up but she got snatched
by a zombie.
"Let go, it's the only way to save yourself!" she shouted.
Reluctantly I did and ran for my life.

Luke Alexander Kyriakou (11)
Llanishen High School, Llanishen

The Enemy Within

Where can I find refuge? Everywhere I turn, it is there. Screaming insults. "You're worthless!" "You're an idiot!" "Everyone hates you!" The unrelenting barrage sears them into my consciousness. Hunting me down until I'm cowering in the corner, dripping with sweat, unable to catch my breath. It attacks. There's no peace, even in my dreams. I can't outrun it or hide from it. Why me? Why? I am running, running from myself, trying to forget, but it won't give up. No amount of diligence will conquer it, it will always be there, wherever I go, the unyielding enemy within.

Emily Combellack (13)
Llanishen High School, Llanishen

The Asylum

I heard the sirens wailing. The screams. I stood up and looked outside. People running. Men in orange suits, bearing bloodstained weapons. Bats. Knives. I darted outside, into the chaos. Then I noticed it. The asylum in the distance, engulfed in flames.

"Run!" screamed a man, as he sprinted away. I glanced back at the asylum, and darted in the opposite direction, over the bridge and into the forest. Suddenly I heard a scream and a faint whimpering. The sinister, distorted laugh of a mad disjointed lunatic. He brandished a knife. He charged. I ran for my life...

Jack Irwin (15)
Llanishen High School, Llanishen

It's Behind Me, Isn't It?

I still have nightmares about it. Every single night. My head hurts just thinking about that night.

"Why me?" I ask myself every night, every day. "What did I do to deserve this?" Wait. No! It's happening again... My legs burn with adrenaline, none of which I've ever felt in my life. The breath that was floating through my lungs left me all too soon. The growl echoes through the world, silencing it. I want to, need to turn my head to face my foe, but my body is paralysed. I have lost. My throat aches from screaming. What's next?

Freya Elizabeth Mary Curtis (12)
Llanishen High School, Llanishen

Escape And Capture

She felt as though she was dying. Exhaustion, humiliation and the freezing cold burned at her very being. She was dry heaving. Her entire town, her family, gone. Hopelessness weighed down her soul. There was nothing left for her. All alone in the world. A crack echoed from behind her and she stopped suddenly, as her heart jumped up to her throat. She held in her whimpers. Her back was pressed against a massive stable oak tree. A shot rang into the silence and a tree not a metre to her right was destroyed. *Damn*, she thought. *They've found me...*

Elisabeth Pritchard (14)
Llanishen High School, Llanishen

Escape

"Must... keep... going!" I told myself. I couldn't feel my feet, I was soaked from head to toe. I was running so fast, my lungs couldn't keep up. Those wolves must have been really hungry, following me all the way out here! This couldn't go on much longer, I felt like I was dying of exhaustion. I decided to accept my fate. I stopped in my tracks and waited... I stood there, more confused than a pretzel trying to untwist itself, as they scampered behind me, whimpering like poodles. Before I could think, we were consumed by a massive shadow...

Lucie Ellen Norman (13)
Llanishen High School, Llanishen

Gotcha

Every step took me deeper into the woods. The stars glared at me, branches poking and scratching at my face whilst the freezing wind whipped my cheeks and froze my tears. Black clouds bled into the sky like ink in water. The flurry of snow blurred all my emotions. My heart attempted to jailbreak from my ribcage, beating violently against my burning chest. I felt a pale hand grip my wrist, nails digging into my flesh, triumphant pride shining in a pair of lifeless eyes. His laugh rumbled like the black clouds closing in on me like a cage. "Gotcha!"

Phoebe Moore (12)
Llanishen High School, Llanishen

The Last Lab Test

They wouldn't find out. How could they? We burnt everything, all our progress, hard work. If we didn't, they would've found out sooner.

"We need to stay off the grid," said the only person who knew, and I can trust. "Get away from our families, everything, disappear. We need to drive, it's not safe for them to know." We drove up to the safe haven in the snowy mountains of Glendale, but when we arrived, the safe house was demolished, a pile of ash in the white snow. They had found out, they knew. How? The chase was now on.

Owen Holcombe (13)
Llanishen High School, Llanishen

Once A Runaway, Always One

I had to dash, now was my time. There was no going back from this. Agents flashed their torches, attempting to find me. This was intense. I knew I couldn't stay here. I was frozen to the bone. Rapidly, I ran into three guns targetting my head, as if I was an alien from Area 51.

"Someone call the boss!" Blood stopped pumping immediately.

This isn't it! I thought to myself. Despite the fact that I had three guns pointing at my head, I had the guts to frantically run and hide. Somehow I managed to escape. I'm so thankful...

Lucas Llwelyn Snow (12)
Llanishen High School, Llanishen

Hunted

The police were after me, the sirens were wailing. I was terrified, there was a group of police flashing their torches in my eyes while I was stumbling through the bushes. I hadn't meant to kill him, he was my friend. The forest howled. I became its prisoner. The days of being carefree had suddenly been stolen by this. The rain was pouring through the twisted trees. There was no light to be seen, the twisted trees were shaking and taunting me. Panic overwhelmed me. I could hear the whirling blades of a hungry helicopter. I was, unfortunately, its victim...

Gethin Enticott (12)
Llanishen High School, Llanishen

Woods

Crash! Aching and sore. Lola was a fair-looking girl, dark brown hair and emerald-green eyes, yet her parents hated her. The abuse, it got too much... Lola suddenly cracked. Slamming open the door and running at an increasing speed, into the woods. Not realising how far she'd gone, she saw darkness. All of a sudden, a tree stump with a demonic carving lit up, illuminating the forest around her. A figure faded in above the stump. Its ocean-green eyes captivated Lola. Its eyes faded to pure black. Liquid oozed down its face. It opened its mouth...

Sophia Chapman (12)
Llanishen High School, Llanishen

Possibilities

I couldn't run for much longer, the oxygen was over-capacitating my lungs immensely. My lungs were as tight as an elastic band. I felt like a mouse running from a ferocious, fearsome lion, ready to maul me. The sirens were raging in the near distance, I almost didn't hear as my heart was thumping like a bass drum. The cannula was still stabbing through my hand, adding incredibly to my intense mental and excruciating physical pain, I couldn't take it a second longer. I reached a bridge, with no way out. I stepped over the railings, gone, into the unknown...

Fearne Williams (15)
Llanishen High School, Llanishen

Anderson Shelter

Stumbling through the dark, misty, mysterious woods, inner voices warn them to go and stay at the same time. No one in their right mind would go in the woods where someone had just died but that didn't stop them, so they stumbled on. Deep in the woods, they began to smell an atrocious smell. They followed the smell and what they found was horrifying! No thirteen-year-old should see what they saw. Traumatised, they ran and ran but it wasn't enough. Dragged by that horrible beast into an abandoned Anderson shelter, they were never ever seen again...

Nia Mohsin (11)
Llanishen High School, Llanishen

Hunted

My heart raced. Sweat poured down my face, drenching every hair it touched. My calves were burning. The piercing scream of the sirens swallowed me. Suddenly, an ice-cold hand seized my wrist. Whoever it was spun me around, but it was too dark to see anything.

"Come with me," a raspy voice whispered. Fear rushed through my body. But for some reason I trusted them. The shadowy figure led me towards a parked car, the headlights were flashing. I didn't see who was driving. We started to drive. Abruptly the car froze. Slowly, my final breath left me...

Fiona Garbutt (12)
Llanishen High School, Llanishen

My Last Chance

Day sixty of the apocalypse. The animals have gone savage and slaughtered all the humans because we destroyed the Earth. So far, everyone is dead. Everyone except me. I, Leah Hunter, am the only human left. Food supplies were running low. I couldn't stay in the city forever. I needed to find somewhere safer. I tried to sneak out of the old Sainsbury's. Slowly I opened the back door, but as I did, a large wolf pounced at me from above. It started ripping clothes and skin. I screamed! I could feel my blood slipping away, escaping my frail body...

Amy Joanne Partridge (11)
Llanishen High School, Llanishen

Lost In Ice Cream

It was midday on Hazelnut Close. James Wilson had gone missing. The police cars with their wailing sirens pulled into the street. I stood by the door, my eyes fixed on the policemen asking the neighbours questions. My mind was racing. How did James manage to disappear only half an hour after I'd seen him through my bedroom window? As I was searching my brain for an answer, a policeman began walking up to me. I started to panic. I didn't have any answers to their questions! But before I could speak, James came around the corner eating ice cream!

Finley Jo Boanas (12)
Llanishen High School, Llanishen

Ripping Free

It was behind me. Grabbing at my neck, it leaned forward and took a bite. I punched its face and ran into the distance, my neck throbbing. I didn't know where I was running to, just away from that. I ran through the village, rain pouring over my wound. I stumbled up the hill, to its home. I stopped outside. The same as before. Still dark. Still gloomy, decaying away. Creaking loudly, the door opened. I went to the kitchen. People's bodies were everywhere! Blood covered the kitchen, floor to ceiling. I turned around. It looked like I was next...

Charley Lewis (12)
Llanishen High School, Llanishen

Experience

I lived in the dense forest of the Amazon rainforest, home to huge biodiversity, where my ancestors lived, after... I don't want to talk about that. All I can say is that they evolved throughout time, becoming higher in the food chain. One morning, I crawled out of the tree canopy. I swung happily through the trees. I stopped, hearing a familiar sound. It was the most strange, upsetting flashback. I turned for a second, seeing an abyss of smoke, I heard the cracking of the tree I was on, but before reaching the ground, I was shot. Reckless beings.

Evan David Peter Johnson (13)
Llanishen High School, Llanishen

The Mission

The sirens wailed. Every dreaded step felt like I was painfully stepping on jagged nails. Panting dogs trailed in my footsteps, on corroded metal chains. Fully-armoured guards fired shots at me. Every time they stopped firing, I thought I was safe. I was awfully wrong. I had already got this far. I couldn't give up, I ploughed through the bushes and when I was safe, I stopped to catch my breath. My mission was almost over. I could hear the whirring engines ahead. I sprinted for my life. I took a massive leap and finally... I was safe now. Forever.

Khalid El-Helaly (13)
Llanishen High School, Llanishen

Escape From Torture

It's not safe now they know where to find me. I had to keep running, no matter how much my body ached. No matter how much the exhaustion was killing me, I couldn't let them find me. The thought of it taunted me. I heard the sirens getting closer and the police dogs barking. I couldn't go back there, I just couldn't. At this point, breathing was painful but I kept going, fuelled by desperation. I couldn't live with the constant experiments they performed on me. The noise of the sirens was getting louder and louder. I felt petrified.

Reema Mohammed (12)
Llanishen High School, Llanishen

Running...

We had one hour to run. We hurried through the big bushy trees, into the suburbs. Bright lights from above blinded us and the noise hurt our ears. They wouldn't find us if we hid behind the supermarket. We knelt down and hoped for the best.

"Are we going to be okay?" she whispered. Sirens flashed and got louder. Lights shone on us like a spotlight. We ran. Into the forest, behind the trees. An army of cars stood outside the woodland. They found us. The apocalypse. It began. We had to get away. Far, where they can't find us...

Polina Patsiakina (13)

Llanishen High School, Llanishen

Run

I still have nightmares about it. I still remember everything: the moonlit path with the jagged rocks, the sirens ringing in my ears. I ran across the path with my head turning very few seconds until no one was in sight and nothing was to be heard except for a dozen squirrels munching acorns. I couldn't run for much longer, so I headed for the woods, where trees towered over you and darkness engulfed your surroundings. I hid behind a splintered log, to rest until I heard the sounds of leaves crunching towards me. Louder and louder... my heart sank.

Rubeen Elgandouz (11)
Llanishen High School, Llanishen

Pursuer

Darkened clouds, void of light, loom over my head. They move like a treadmill, as I sprint forth into the woods ahead. My feet pound against the cold broken ground, pushing me forward, away from my deaded fate. My blank-faced pursuer inches ever closer towards me, like a wolf chasing its prey. Suddenly, like a knife in the night, he reaches out his hand, with an overwhelming grip. Shock paralyses my body, as this creature's hand grabs my right shoulder. I am lashed back in towards the shadow of a great oak tree. Slowly, I lose all feeling...

Finlay White (14)
Llanishen High School, Llanishen

A Corrupt World!

The world was imploding, all reality turning on itself and crushing those who try to stop it. I knew why the men in white took people who knew what they were doing, and soon I was next. Their toxic games toying with reality, making freedom sound like a punishment. They were here, outside my house, just out of reach. The heavy footsteps of the men in white like alarm bells in my ears.
Run away! I thought, knowing that I would be doomed anyway, just another pawn on their corrupt chessboard. My final end loomed... I had been hunted.

Evie Price (11)
Llanishen High School, Llanishen

The Chase

I couldn't run for much longer. Sweat dripping down my face, I tried to find a clearing amongst the trees. Where could I hide? I scrambled through the bushes, brambles scratching along my legs and arms. Gasping for air, I reached a cave. Crawling through the opening, I sat on the damp, cold floor of the pitch-black cave. Drinking out of a puddle, I planned my escape route. And that's when the siren started. The sound became louder and then it stopped. The silence felt like an eternity. Until a spotlight shone down the cave. I needed to escape!

Ellie Exintaris (15)
Llanishen High School, Llanishen

Hunted

All around me were dead bodies. The people I had slaughtered were a threat to me and my clan. As I limped through the hallways I saw a black figure in front of me. I crept forward, and suddenly the lights switched on. Then came the hunters.

"We've found her!" I dashed through the hallway, seeking an exit. I needed to escape. They couldn't find where my clan were. If they captured me, they could use me to their advantage against them. I felt so tired and corrupted. Then a flash of light came into my view. I leapt, shivering.

Shyane Li (14)

Llanishen High School, Llanishen

Hunted

My legs were shaking, getting weaker. I made it, to the road with so many trees. A car came past and splashed me. I spilt out on to the road. Another car was coming. Time froze...
The car stopped and a person got out of the car.
"Hi! Have you been running for a while?" I didn't answer, I looked at the ground and nodded. "Get in the car then, I will help you."
I got into the car, not saying anything. "I'm... one of you. Don't worry, I will save you." He drove off.
I was saved...

Heidi Cleverley (11)
Llanishen High School, Llanishen

Hunted

The crouching beast in the long grass. Waiting, staring...
running! The adrenaline rushed through my veins. The bird
escaped... I carried on searching for my next target. My first
attempt for a catch failed. I was only just warming up... I
saw a bunch of birds perched on the edge of my jungle's
fence. I slowly crept towards them using grass as cover.
They were only a few metres away. I could get them.
"Kylo?" Oh no, it was my horrible owner, Ben. "Come here
Kylo." He grabbed me and took me inside. "You're the
peskiest cat ever Kylo!"

Ben Richmond (13)
Llanishen High School, Llanishen

Smile

The screams made it sound like there were hundreds of them, but in reality, there were four. Well, three now. I looked up from the body, their eyes revealing their fear, they ran. Slowly, I smiled. I started walking, my smile growing wider with each passing second. I walked into the dusty room at the end of the hallway. It was dark, but I heard them shaking in the corner of the room. Three... two... one. They were gone. My smile was wider than ever, as the blood trickled away. But I'm not done yet, there's still one victim left...

Caitlin Ruby Clarke (13)
Llanishen High School, Llanishen

Birthday Present?

It had to be here somewhere! Mel and I had been looking everywhere. Looking for that valuable item Mel had been sent for her birthday. Mel and I are sisters, we had a strange phone call on her fifteenth birthday and now we're on a hunt to find her long-lost treasure. We know it's in the enchanted forest, but the only problem is, it's surrounded by pixies, magical evil creatures that can spell you to death. Off we went, to search for Mel's treasure. We were close, but we only had twenty-four hours to get past 3000 pixies...

Danae Eugenia Roberts (11)

Llanishen High School, Llanishen

The Gift

With no knowledge of where I was going, I kept running and running, but I was going nowhere. With my beating heart bursting through my chest, I came to a halt. The golden necklace was finally in my grasp. But suddenly they were surrounding me, from every angle possible. Searching for a way out I heard the sirens and accepted the reality - I had been caught. Herding towards me with cuffs, my hands were snatched. That's when I jumped. I was awake. Christmas had arrived. And so had Santa and his reindeers with my gift of the golden necklace.

Emma Jones (16)
Llanishen High School, Llanishen

You Can Run, But You Can't Hide

The moonlight reflected off the lake as I ran through the field, my heart pounding and my eyes darting around, scanning for a hiding place. The towering figure getting bigger as it got closer. Soon, the ground changed to the squeaky wooden planks of an old jetty. I ran to the end of it with the wind slapping my face. At the water's edge, I found a rusty old speedboat bobbing up and down. I unwrapped the rope with frostbitten hands and started the engine. It drifted away from the jetty. The figure just stood there, it didn't follow me...

Logan Shahwan (13)
Llanishen High School, Llanishen

Guilty

I did it. And they know that, and I did it for a good reason too. She disrespected me. She didn't realise what I was capable of. Do you know what the funny thing is? I don't regret it. I laughed with joy when she was confirmed dead. I warned her, what was she expecting? The Monster of Atlantic College, that's what they call me. I'm a monster because I killed *one* person? I mean, that's one less person to spend money on, one less person to care about, one less person to deal with. They should be thanking me...

Lydia Francis (14)
Llanishen High School, Llanishen

The Clown Chase!

I had twenty-four hours until the clown stopped chasing me. I jumped over a fence and hid behind a dumpster. I could hear it calling my name. "Georgie, come out!" My friend found me and shouted, "Hey, over here!" I ran over and tried to run home as fast as possible until we reached a dead end. He was walking towards us slowly. He had razor-sharp teeth and a dagger in his hand, he crept further until *bang*, he had been shot from behind. "Dad!" I shouted.
"Hurry up, boys!" he replied. We ran away before the clown came back.

Mia Roberts (11)
Llanishen High School, Llanishen

My End

We were close, but yet again, so far. As I'm sprinting faster than before I can just feel them behind me. I know they're behind me. I still have nightmares about it. Nightmares about how I got here, why I'm trapped here. I can remember them chasing me and me remembering I couldn't run much longer. My legs aching, thinking of just giving up. But yet again I couldn't, my life was depending on it. Here I am, trapped, trapped inside a cell with two psychopaths, trapping us inside. Inside until the end, the very end, with the psychopaths...

Amelia Bebb (12)
Llanishen High School, Llanishen

Two Ways To Die

Running, panting, sweating. The demon was chasing me. It had two blood-red eyes, two horns, blood dripping from one. Colossal in size, covered in black dirty wool, it had lots of cuts and bruises. Then there were two paths. Right or left, which one? I panicked. In a flash, I chose right. Then I encountered another beast, its tail was dropping at low speed. I wasn't going to make it. I slid for it and made it by a whisker. The demon charged and knocked over the beast. I was in pursuit.

How would I survive? A cliff. I jumped...

Shivajith K Pandian (11)

Llanishen High School, Llanishen

Moonlight

Dashing, running, my vision blurred. Where was it? Was it behind or in front? A lake was ahead so I headed in that direction. The lake reflected the moonlight like a crystal waterfall. *Klunk!* The whir of Servos drew closer... Its eyes illuminated the lake as if it had spotlights in its eyes. Testing the water, I hesitantly jumped into the lake. There was no way it could follow me into the lake, right? Like a leviathan it chased me, but its jaw was locked shut. When I reached the air, it did too, and when it did, it changed...

Jacob Nuno Levy Parsons (12)

Llanishen High School, Llanishen

Extremely Good Looking

The man was killed in broad daylight, a heartless show of power. Wanted sheets spread across the street, no face upon them. Nobody knows who he is, but he will strike again. I pictured the man, a mangled mess left to die. There was no saving him. Kidneys missing. We took him to his family, end of victim one. Every criminal file searched, no one kills as this man does. In a way, he's special. Another call, another victim. A woman, another mangled mess, liver missing and unrecognisable. No one knows who he is, but he will strike again.

Maazin Rizwan (11)
Llanishen High School, Llanishen

On The Run

Endless days. Sleepless nights. It couldn't get any worse. The incident that occurred has left me scarred for life. It's that time of the month to go and see the most precious person in my life. My mum! She's been admitted ever since that day. As a single mother, you can imagine how hard it might be to make ends meet. We have been on the run for five years now. Just imagine! Running away from insurance companies, debt collectors and all sorts. Our lives are meaningless now. I question her to this day. Why did you do this?

Tasmia Mamun (13)
Llanishen High School, Llanishen

The Coffin

The sirens wailed! Wind blew! I was trapped. Was I dead?
No! Where am I? Is it heaven? No, it reeks too much. I yelled!
I screeched! It was no use. I couldn't be heard by
anyone. *Stomp! Clatter!* Footsteps!
"Help, I'm trapped!" And that was when I realised where I
was. A coffin! But I was alive. I was trapped in someone's
body! Not forever, right? That can't be. I was in a graveyard!
"Help!" I was on my own. Scared and freezing to death.
Literally. Will I ever be free? That's a question for the future
to answer...

Ella James (11)
Llanishen High School, Llanishen

The Hospital

I sprinted through the dimly lit hall. There was a bin, a blanket-covered chair, and a box. Where to hide? They burst open the door. There was someone shining a torch at me. I removed the tattered blanket and climbed up the square metal vent. As I crawled through, it was getting darker. *Clunk!* I was as quiet as I could be. I dropped down from the vent. It was an abandoned hospital. I looked at the overgrown walls. They were covered in blood. I had a weird feeling in my stomach. *Crash!* I ran for the door. Locked...

Dylan Camilleri (12)
Llanishen High School, Llanishen

Hunted

Broken: a world full of fire, smoke and ash. It's survival of the fittest. This was once home. An insect-like man with his boy was wandering around looking for anything to salvage. One day maybe this world would reignite. It might get better. My arms, claws, fingertips, were cold. My boy and I were limping down the wasteland's demolished road. Dead trees had fallen across it a long time ago. My boy and I were walking through what was once a forest until we saw something in the distance. What was it? We'd go to find out together...

Latrell Wilson (15)
Llanishen High School, Llanishen

Soaring

Cool air calms my pounding fears. My legs feel like jelly. This is the most foolish, yet important thing I have ever done. Nervously, I look down at the thirty-foot drop. I have to go before I change my mind. If this goes wrong, I will die but if I don't, my soul won't survive. I leap, run and fall. Seagulls soar alongside me, talking to me through piercing shrieks, fierce waves crash beneath me, a jumbled coast vaguely familiar. Why am I doing this? My hang-glider rustles forcefully. I have to find her... the hunt is on.

Ella Crockford (12)
Llanishen High School, Llanishen

Hunted!

The sirens wailed. What have I done? I walked into the dingy forest. I could hear voices saying to me, "Killer!" Oh, the sirens were getting closer. I ran. I could not run much longer. The storm was getting much worse, so I ran into a nearby cave. It was just me, the darkness, and my thoughts. Well, that's just what I thought. Until I heard a rumble, wait, was that an earthquake? What was that? I started to panic. I started to question why I have the right to live. Should I? I have just murdered an innocent child...

Mia Jean Sturla (12)
Llanishen High School, Llanishen

A Daring Escape

My body hurting, I had only narrowly escaped the grasp of my captor and was already doubting whether I could outrun him. It was a catastrophic escape and I consequently had a gaping hole through my leg, limiting my movement. Dogs barking alerted me to their presence nearby, blood dripping from my leg wasn't helping so I made the decision to wade my way through the river, to drop my scent. After hours of tiring running, I decided it was time to rest. I found a log to rest in. Footsteps right outside alerted me, had they found me?

Dylan Morgan (15)
Llanishen High School, Llanishen

Hunted By Boys

Sirens wailed all around me as I was running to safety. My heart was racing out of my chest. I couldn't run for much longer, footsteps behind me were already getting closer. I had to run. Now. I had no choice. They were too close. I knew I couldn't stop but I had to. My legs and my chest were in agony. I only stopped for two seconds in the woods, all alone. All of a sudden I was surrounded by a gang of boys.

"Help!" I screeched from the top of my lungs.

"Sssh... you're one of us now..."

Macey Williams (13)
Llanishen High School, Llanishen

The Capture

I couldn't run for much longer... my legs ached and my chest burned. But I couldn't stop. If I did, they would catch me. They always find a way. The bright shining of headlights caught my eye. A horrible feeling rushed through me as I trudged through the autumn leaves, trying to be mute. I heard the tyres of a substantial Range Rover. The voices of the capture following me, mentally and physically. I suddenly felt cold hands wrap around my waist and cover my mouth. I was back, shackled to the walls until I had another chance...

Isabelle Evans-Boon (12)
Llanishen High School, Llanishen

The Woman

I stared up from my bed. I was terrified. *Crash!* There it was! It sounded like it was coming from the kitchen downstairs. I rushed out of my bed and grabbed my knife. I secretly hid under my bed. Whilst I was doing that, I heard the sound of footsteps from heels coming towards my room. My heart skipped a beat. I quickly headed to my wardrobe and waited there. The woman smashed open the door and headed for the wardrobe. I covered my mouth with my hands. *Creak!* The door slowly opened... *Creak, creak...*

Nirushni Sudhakar (11)
Llanishen High School, Llanishen

Lost And Found

Fear shivered down my spine. I was trapped. My legs trailed behind as I ran through the glacial snow. I had to keep going. In the distance, a piercing noise was heading towards me. I was trapped. Ahead I could see a gloomy forest. Running in, I didn't know what to expect. As the screech was continuous, some powerful looking men meandered up to me. They surrounded me like a pack of starving wolves. Creeping closer my shaky legs started to feel like they were going to collapse. But then it all changed. I was here, safe at home!

Sophie Baines (11)
Llanishen High School, Llanishen

World War III

The day was bright, not a single problem at all, until the sirens started to blare, signifying that the Soviets had crossed the airspace and were dropping bombs. There was a big plane, bigger than the others. A black object flew from the bottom of the plane, zooming down at a thousand miles per hour. It struck the ground. The floor shook as I looked up to see a mushroom cloud. I stared for ten seconds then sprinted towards the shelter. The blast radius travelled through the air. It reached my house as I got to the shelter...

Ethan Bebb (13)

Llanishen High School, Llanishen

The Escape

The robbery had gone wrong and I knew I had to get off the grid, or I'd die in prison. Quickly I got to my car and heard helicopters and sirens getting louder. My foot on the accelerator, my car jumped to sixty miles-per-hour. I glanced at my mirror and saw four police cruisers. I drove through the cities motorways. I had to get to the forest, that was my best chance of escaping. I roared off to the side after twenty minutes of pursuit. Quickly I went into the forest, hiding from civilisation forever, never to be seen again.

Ardit Bullatovci (13)
Llanishen High School, Llanishen

Hunted

It wasn't safe to stay here, we needed to go now. They were coming. My arms and feet were shaking, it felt like I was on fire. They were banging on the door. I opened the frosty window and climbed down the unsteady drain pipe, down into the claustrophobic back garden. This felt like a parallel universe, there was nowhere to go now. My head was ringing, I had not eaten or drunk all day. They had cornered us off. We were stuck, the end was coming, we had to surrender. Then the noise of the PS4 turned off. "Mum!"

Alfie Perriam (12)
Llanishen High School, Llanishen

Border Run

I had ten minutes to get to the border and escape for good. The siren started - I'd become the prey. I began sprinting as fast as an Olympic runner, hoping to make some distance between me and my hunters. I kept going, amazed at my pace and stamina, which I had seemed to have developed out of nowhere. I could hear them getting closer, their distinct panting and spine-chilling roar. I knew I had to get off the ground - somewhere up high where they could not pounce on me and take me in again. I had to get away, finally...

Issy Wilce (15)
Llanishen High School, Llanishen

The Best Christmas

I woke up, over the moon, It was Christmas morning. My sister was bouncing on my bed, screaming with excitement. We both ran upstairs to wake up our exhausted parents. Yanking our stockings, we heaved them onto the bed. As a pair of knives appeared, so did bars of metal, followed by bows and arrows. As my parents opened their presents, joy grew in their eyes. An incredible day was on the horizon! We quickly got kitted up and left the house in search of turkey. Once our prey was spotted, we would hunt it for the best dinner!

Seren Carson (16)
Llanishen High School, Llanishen

The Horrible Haunted House

It has to be here somewhere, I thought, wandering around the wicked woods. The treacherous trees had faces as scary as monsters and the woods were filled with noises and sounds, like the trees were moaning. I was out late, looking for the horrible haunted house. It only appears at night, since that is the only time that the ghosts come out. There it was, in the distance, the dreaded house! I sprinted as fast as a racecar to see the inside. To my surprise, I just saw an old man and an old woman, having a cup of tea!

Joshua Bryn Nelson-Piney (12)
Llanishen High School, Llanishen

Jail Break

I've been in here for seven years now, I got arrested for manslaughter. I need to break out, my wife is annoyed because we have three kids and they're too hard to handle. I told my wife I'm going to break out tonight and she's going to be waiting. I've got the perfect plan. There's a hole in the roof. It's the night of the escape, I'm so close to getting out. I climb out. Finally! I see my wife. We're going to flee to Mexico together to start a new life, we're leaving tonight...

Elle-May Lewis
Llanishen High School, Llanishen

Hunted

Sirens wailed as I dashed with the world behind my back. All I could hear was the screaming sound of the helicopter. I couldn't run for much longer. All of a sudden I felt a bullet fly behind me. Fear was twisting throughout my brain, but when I was finally safe, I heard a whisper. "Hello, Subject 516234." My body stopped. I was regretting my decision. A man in the same rags as me repeated, "Hello Subject 516234."
I mumbled, "Um... um... hello? How do you know my name?" *Bang!* A gunshot went through my body.

Martin Carter (11)

Llanishen High School, Llanishen

Hunted

The sirens wailed. My heart was beating quickly. I didn't mean what I did. It wasn't my fault. I saw the dead body lying in front of me. I didn't know what to do. My head was spinning. They were catching up to me. Panic coursed through my veins, or was it fear? My white robe caught a branch and I fell to the ground. When I woke up, I was in a place I didn't recognise, a mysterious place. There were people all around me, police officers, doctors. The sirens wailed. My heart was beating. I'd been hunted.

Eva Violet Court (12)
Llanishen High School, Llanishen

Sweet And Sticky

The sirens wailed. The helicopter whirled above my head.
The hunt was on. Feelings invaded my mind; was I regretting
this decision? Should I return? The smell of the fresh bread
from the bakery encouraged me to keep moving. All of a
sudden, I heard a car come hurtling around a corner. I threw
myself into a ditch and kept down. As I sat in the mud, all I
could think about was the sweet smell of the cinnamon-
infused doughy prize that I was heading for. As I peered
across the road, I could see it: the insignificant marker!

Ruben James Kelman (12)
Llanishen High School, Llanishen

Hunted

We were floating through the air until the driver sneezed and his knees knocked the steering wheel. This made the plane slope downwards, I hit the emergency button. So when we landed, we all leapt out of the plane and ran. I tried to follow everyone but I lost them within seconds. I stopped and heard someone talking. Then, out of the bushes came the children off the plane. We found a clearing because we thought it would be easier for people to find us. A plane landed to fly us back and everyone was happy to see us home.

Phoebe Hopson (11)
Llanishen High School, Llanishen

The Demon From The Portal Of Hell

I thought I believed in curses, apparently not. It was a blustery and frosty night and I was in my bed, watching TV as usual. My mum was making delicious milk and white chocolate brownies. Mmm. I suddenly heard an echo from downstairs. I didn't know what it was but I was frightened. I decided to get out of bed, adrenaline was flowing through my veins. I noticed something strange; the lights were off and there was graffiti on the walls. I closed my eyes and prepared for the unexpected. A demon stood in front of me...

Oliver Barnett (13)
Llanishen High School, Llanishen

The Big Game

Cold. Wet. Shivering. It was the last ten minutes of the final of the Welsh Cup. *Screeech*. The sound of the ref's whistle pierced my ears as he blew for a penalty against us. Their kicker stepped up to touch the ball. Line-out twenty-two. The ball was thrown into the line-out like a bullet from a gun. The ball was then tossed out to the backs. Quickly, I ran forward and plucked the ball from the air. Furiously, I hurtled towards their try line. It felt like I was being hunted in the woods. Would I make it?

Ben Weare
Llanishen High School, Llanishen

Hide-And-Seek!

I couldn't hide for much longer. I had to stop running. My stomach was cartwheeling. I felt like I was on a never-ending roller coaster that didn't stop doing crazy loops. Suddenly I heard a petrifying scream behind me. Cautiously, I turned around but nothing was there! It was just a pitch-black, narrow street. I turned back around and started to run again. Suddenly, I felt a pain in my back. I fell headfirst onto the ground. Slowly, I rolled over and all I saw was vicious red eyes glaring at me in the dark street...

Paris Leaman (11)
Llanishen High School, Llanishen

Hunted

Blood dripping down the knife wound, I scream in excruciating pain. My life is flashing before my eyes. Violent images of the stabbing replay in my mind over and over. I'm as stiff as a statue, lifeless like a ghost. The staggering pain forcefully pumping around my body. I lie in a pitch-black alley. I black out. Seeing my life one more time before I flat line, I see a familiar face: my best friend. I realised he was my attacker. My last thought, *why would my best friend stab me?* Don't trust anyone.

Dre Day (15)
Llanishen High School, Llanishen

Where Am I?

I still have nightmares about it. The day they came for me. Their voices still echo in my ears like ghosts in a haunted mansion. The thought of them ever coming back shook me to the core, sending chills down my spine. I remember running for my life, making every step count. I was dizzy and tired. Dizzy. Tired. Darkness. I passed out with exhaustion, my knees dropped to the floor and my hand scraped painfully across the rough, dirty concrete. I awoke in a cold, dusky, dimly lit basement where I was tied to a chair...

Farah Elise Thomas (12)
Llanishen High School, Llanishen

The Haunted House

There was a boy called Max who was stranded in a haunted house. There were a lot of red bloody balloons scattered around the room. Suddenly there was something wandering around the haunted house. It came closer and closer with a balloon in front of its face. It carefully moved the balloon out of the way. Max was surprised at how evil it looked. It had a white silvery top and two red bloody marks on its face. Max was scared and ran out of the haunted house. The clown chased him through the forest with a chainsaw...

Max Gardener (11)
Llanishen High School, Llanishen

Time

I couldn't go on for much longer. Twenty-four hours had taken its toll, my back had shooting pains and my head was pounding. I looked up. No moon or stars. I saw a dim glow across the lake. It seemed half-human, half-horse! Suddenly it started to charge, I couldn't hear it though. A tree fell over behind me. I fumbled for my rifle but couldn't find it. Where was my stuff? The animal wasn't stopping! My life flashed before me, questions I was burning to ask! Like why was the animal glowing? I glimpsed the animal...

Naina Luchmun (12)

Llanishen High School, Llanishen

The Invasion

It landed on the ground. They emerged from their pod. We ran but not all of us could escape them. We worried as we heard screams from the other side of the barricades. My eyes flashed, then my best friend was gone. The greeny-blueish things had lots of us. What happened to them? I don't know. But I knew it wasn't good. Then they found me. I sprinted as far as possible but they caught me. As I went in, I saw them all. In tubes, they were lying dead. I didn't worry anymore. This was the alien invasion...

Joel Matthew White (12)

Llanishen High School, Llanishen

Chased!

Snap! I spun my head around. My eyes scanned the never-ending forest. My senses heightened ever since I escaped from the awful hellhole they had kept me captive in for the last four years., I was a government secret, and they wanted me back.

"Over here!" I heard a shout from the distance. I started sprinting as fast as my legs would allow. I was so close to the border, where I would be safe. There's no way I'm allowing them to take me back. I felt a sharp pain in my neck, and the world went dark...

Alisha White (14)
Llanishen High School, Llanishen

The Nightmare

My legs burned like fire and every breath I took was torture. My heart was pounding like a herd of wild rhinos. Then the wailing of the sirens came, I was captured. Blue and white lights blinded me. They drove me back to the grim old place, cold and lonely, the grey walls taunting me as I was escorted back to my cell. I knew my life was never going to be perfect and I knew that was my fault. If only I could re-write history... My eyelids fluttered in the early morning sunshine.

"Oh!" It was all a nightmare!

Katie Gardener (12)
Llanishen High School, Llanishen

The Walking Dead

I stood motionless. They were green, with blood dripping from their mouths, eager for human flesh. I ran without looking back. I snuck into an abandoned warehouse, hoping someone would find me. I hid behind a load of crates and ducked. I was there for a while so I decided to take a look around. After about an hour of looking, I found a baseball bat and some survival supplies. What was that? There was a knock at the door. At first, I thought I was saved, but I was charged by a horde of zombies. It was too late...

Rhys James Christopher Haines (13)
Llanishen High School, Llanishen

School Of Hell

I'm sprinting, panting, like a lion hunting down its prey. I hastily peer behind me, only to see a stumbling, hungry, flesh-devouring zombie, blood trickling from its mouth. It licks it up without hesitation. I leap like a gazelle onto the next building. Unfortunately, I fall and twist my ankle but before I know it, I feel an excruciating pain in my leg. Blood splatters on my face. I lick it off. My eyes are wide and I roar loudly. From the corner of my eye, I see a scrumptious piece of meat. They're going down!

Holly Gentle (15)
Llanishen High School, Llanishen

Quiet Place

I couldn't run much longer. My legs shaking, my heart beating faster. I was sweating so much, it was like a huge cloud just rained water on me. I could see my friend suffering. We ran into a hospital to find help. The hospital looked like it was abandoned. We looked for something to use but there was nothing. We went to one room to see what we could find, we took a couple of steps inside while the floor rotted. We looked down to see the floor rot then *bang!* We looked back at the door, it shut quickly...

Sammy Kaur (11)
Llanishen High School, Llanishen

On The Run

We had to leave, now, before we got caught. They were coming, the army of children was coming. What had they done to them? We ran down to the abandoned school as the sirens wailed, killing our ears. They've taken over our friends, it's like they controlled their brains. To be honest, we had bigger problems. What about eating, drinking, or even seeing our families? From out of nowhere, *bang, boom, crash!* The wall came crumbling down. They caught us. What should we do? Would we become one of them?

Charlotte Emily Picton (11)

Llanishen High School, Llanishen

One Of Us

I shot up, knowing that I needed to run. I could hear gunshots from every direction, pieces of dirt flying around me from the explosions and grenades and tanks. I kept running until I made it to the forest with a face full of scratches, blood dripping from my arm onto my hand. As I thought I was clear I heard someone shout.
"Quick, he went that way!" My heart raced. I looked backwards, they were getting closer. Finally, they caught up to me. He turned me around and saw my flag.
"Guys, he's one of us!"

Harvey Herring (11)
Llanishen High School, Llanishen

The Happy Never Ending

The sirens wailed. The rumours were true. The secret was let out, now everyone knew Levie was killed. It wasn't safe now they knew where he lived. I had to get there before they found out they were close to the truth. We had twenty-four hours to find the man and kill him otherwise we would be killed and that would be the end of our country. We didn't have much time to crack the case. We got to the house, no one was there. Silence. Until we went into the basement and saw everyone's worst nightmare imaginable...

Nikita Macintosh (12)
Llanishen High School, Llanishen

Beast

I could not run for much longer. I could hear the riot I had started. The sirens roared through the town, looking for me. I made it. To the woods. And that's when I saw it. A miniature dark beast staring into my eyes. It started walking, jogging, running towards me. I ran for my life. Down towards the river. Then I had a sensation roller-coastering down my leg. It was a pain. Suddenly, I tumbled down to the river's edge and stopped right on the edge. Then I saw it again, the beast with dark red eyes...

Elli Roberts
Llanishen High School, Llanishen

Bianca

"Run!" I remembered that word as we ran. We destroyed the transmitter. They were after us. Thousands of us had died. There was a safe camp for the children somewhere, or so they said. I was only fifteen. Me and the boys were a few miles away. We stole the gun and weapons. We killed them, destroyed them, broke them. But still, they come. I named them Bianca. The name of a girl I'd hated as a child. The last thing I remember seeing was the inside of Bianca's mouth. After that, it was all black!

Rahan Mankoor (15)
Llanishen High School, Llanishen

The Hunted

I couldn't run any longer. My legs were beginning to let me down. I stumbled over a root and fell into a tree. I heard their shouts. They were close. How could I get away? My legs had given way and could no longer support my body. I was to be caught and taken for trial.

"This is the end," I muttered to myself.

"Psst...climb up!" A voice whispered from the trees above. I didn't hesitate. Looking back I could see the torches peering through the trees.

"You'll be safe here, they won't find you..."

Noah Barton (12)
Llanishen High School, Llanishen

Trapped

I had to leave. Now. I was in pain, unable to breathe. Everything was so tight, my body was burning. I didn't remember anything that had happened. Waking up to bugs swarming around my body was unexpected. I knew I had been drugged. I should have believed my mother. I should have stayed home. I kicked and pushed as hard as I could, reached out for my phone for light, but it was drained. This was it. There was no other solution. This was the end. Wait! Someone was coming. Was it help, or was this the end of me?

Manar El-Kaddu (15)
Llanishen High School, Llanishen

The Escape

The sirens wailed. In that split second, I knew I had to escape. My heart sank, the police were coming after me. "They framed me!" I shouted. I decided to run. I didn't even know where I was going. All I knew was that I had to follow my feet. After a while, I couldn't hear the sirens anymore. I waited until the crack of dawn in a bush. When they finally went past me I jumped over the fence and then came to a halt. A dead end... What was I supposed to do? I heard something. They were here...

Evie Malcolm-Ward (12)

Llanishen High School, Llanishen

Mission Space

She'd disappeared, leaving a note that said, 'I'm somewhere in space, you have twenty-fours to find me. If you fail, you die! Your time starts now.' I grabbed the phone and started ringing everyone I knew, but I was just wasting time. I started looking for scraps to build some sort of ship. Finished! It took eight hours. Then it was time to go up into space. As I went up, my skin started to bubble and burn, I started to feel sick. I wasn't going to make it. The ship was going to explode!

Eliza Davies (12)

Llanishen High School, Llanishen

Choices

The gates clunked as they unlocked and swept open before me. I didn't have long. I scanned the clearing that spanned out, looking for hiding spots. In ten minutes, the beast will come to find me. If I can't hide, I'm done for. There was a cave on my left - too risky, there might not be a way back out. There was a forest in front, there would be more cover but I doubt that matters against this apex predator. There was a maze to my right, I could spend time getting myself lost there. Sirens blared. Too late.

Callum Tucker (15)
Llanishen High School, Llanishen

The Nugget Monster

I had twenty-four hours to get back to base with the nuggets for our new cave. Bad thing is, the FBI were called and the heist was cut short.

"Oh no!" They had found us. All I heard was gunshots behind me. Half of my squad was wiped out. I yelled, "Deploy the mechs!" We got back safely (well, some of us did). We dumped the nuggets down and jumped. Then I saw it.

"Run!" Bob yelled. Its arms the size of trucks. Its teeth as sharp as daggers. It killed all but two of us. Me and Bob. "Charge!"

Jack Flowers (11)
Llanishen High School, Llanishen

The Creepy Maze!

We have to leave because there's a creepy, slow and loud alien trying to eat me. But I can't get out, because I'm stuck in the maze. There's got to be a way out. As I turn around, I see a guy.

I say, "Hello, can you hear me?" When he turns around, I scream because he is not a human. He is an alien! He turns green and looks gross and scary. He has sharp teeth.

He says, "Weahowadro!"

I reply, "What does that mean?" He repeats it again and again.

Dylan Richard Edwards (11)
Llanishen High School, Llanishen

The Game Where No One Survives

I became the prey of the most violent game humanity could play. I woke up and I was chained up to a metal pole in the middle of the woods, with a big thick metal collar around my neck, like a dog. I tried to move but the metal chain was too short and kept pulling me back to the pole. Suddenly, I heard footsteps crunching on crunchy leaves. I saw a big, buff, muddy man coming towards me, swinging a machete around and around repeatedly until he reached me. Suddenly, he broke me from my chain and we ran...

Jessica Symons (15)
Llanishen High School, Llanishen

Halloween

It was a dark Halloween night. Two boys called Jack and Max decided to go trick or treating. They had got a whole pillowcase full of sweets so they decided to go to just one more house. Max had a bad feeling that something was going to happen, but he didn't know what. Then Max saw a girl with black hair and ragged clothes. Max shouted, "Run!" and they both ran like there was no tomorrow. They told their mum everything. She called the police. The police tried to find the girl but found no trace of her...

Ruby Diggins (11)
Llanishen High School, Llanishen

Hunted

I can't hide any longer, they are always searching. In a world where werewolves used to exist. I am the last of my kind. Every full moon I turn into a werewolf. I'm getting chased by some secret service, I hear they want to turn me into one of their test subjects. I don't really know who my parents are. I do know that the other wolves raised me, taught me how to survive. Last night they chased me far away until I found my wolf friends. I ran with them and eventually, we lost track of the secret service.

Hana Davies (11)
Llanishen High School, Llanishen

Hunted

The owls hooted loudly. It was dark and gloomy. I couldn't see anything, there was a murderer chasing after me. At one point, I couldn't breathe. Suddenly, I saw him and I ran to a hiding spot. I found a spot in a tree. He walked past me several times, circling the area. I didn't want to make a single noise, just in case he saw me. I could not stay in the tree for much longer. My legs were slipping... I fell out. He saw me. I tried running but I was out of breath. There were lights ahead...

Oliver Selby (12)
Llanishen High School, Llanishen

Doom

There I was, running for my life. I couldn't run much longer so I looked behind me and I thought I lost it. So, I stopped. Suddenly I heard a whistle. Coming closer, I started to panic. My heart was pounding out of my chest, I glared at it in fear. A red-eyed, bloodthirsty killer! Anxiety sweating through me, I ran. I tried to escape. I couldn't. I kept running. I saw a road and my car! I turned around. "Aaargh!" I looked at the murderer and in his hands was my best friend... dead. Frightened, I ran...

Harley Dudley (11)
Llanishen High School, Llanishen

The Shortcut

I couldn't run much longer. We chose to take a shortcut through the woods. Many children have gone into the woods and never returned. Ahead of me was the end of the woods. I suddenly froze on the spot. A few steps ahead of me was a clown, under a lamp post that was flickering. All I could do was sprint past the clown. As soon as I started sprinting the clown chased after me. I sprinted faster and jumped into a bush nearby. Then I realised my best friend and I had split up. I never saw him again...

Ffion Rankin (11)

Llanishen High School, Llanishen

I'm Not A Number

I can't take it anymore. I was just an experiment to them. Number 76392. I had twenty-four hours, I had to leave now. Panting heavily, legs aching, stomach hurting, I couldn't do this anymore, but I knew that if I gave up I would go back to just being a number. I can't let that happen, so I moved forward until I saw some lights from the nearest highway. Suddenly, the leaves crunched behind me, but there was no one there. I walked forward to exit the forest. Today my life changed forever...

Kiara Thomas (13)
Llanishen High School, Llanishen

Help Me

My legs were on fire. I was drowning in my own sweat and tears. My whole body was burning. I felt like somebody was smashing me with a huge metal hammer. I could hear loud booming sirens in the distance. Tall men dressed in black were closing in on me in all directions, and there were lights blinding me. I stumbled on, not knowing where the hell I was going or what was happening to me. All of a sudden I could feel huge rough hands clamped over my bloody mouth. I was gasping for air.
"Help me!"

Imogen Hughes (12)
Llanishen High School, Llanishen

Hunted

Another light flickered, a text that read 'Time is ticking, you have twenty hours left. By the end of this, I want my money. If not, your life will become a living hell!' My body shivered. Was it a joke or was it serious? Who sent it? Why did they send it? Do they even know who they're speaking to? Panicking, I was walking up and down the corridor, what do they want from me? Eleven hours left. Didn't even have half of the money. All of a sudden an alarm started buzzing on my phone. I ran, and fast!

Macy Watson (13)
Llanishen High School, Llanishen

My Mission

It was my mission and nobody was going to stop me. I charged forwards, but before I knew it, an acid shower hit. It burned my skin. I kept running for what felt like hours until I came across hideous creatures, some old, some young, many handing out pieces of homework to a swarm of zombies. Soon I was swept away by the swarm, but I got away. I climbed the highest mountain and at the peak was an item, my ball. I was probably getting detention but I was an unlikely hero, and they were hunting me...

Jasmine Lee (11)
Llanishen High School, Llanishen

The Broken Runaway

I couldn't run for much longer. My feet burned from running, my chest was numb, my hands were frozen from the cold. I had to keep moving or I'd be dead. They were coming for me and if I stopped, they would find me. I just needed to disappear. I slipped, my leg got caught on a branch. I could hear them. I panicked as I tried to free myself. I was too late. I ducked my head and looked away. They could smell my human blood from a mile away. I looked up for less than a second. *Crack!*

Lana Hembury (12)
Llanishen High School, Llanishen

What Am I?

No one will know who I am. Because there is nobody here but me. Once the dust settles and the sirens stop wailing, I will embark on my quest for vengeance. Although maybe not. There is no one here! I don't know how long I've been here, my vision has only just returned but there is not much around. Sand, that's all that's near. I don't know where I am and I don't know if I'm in danger. Then, a hand reaches out. It is a man.

"I am one of you," he muffles.

"But what am I?" Silence grows.

Thalia Lewis-Foran (15)
Llanishen High School, Llanishen

You Will Be Found

I had to leave now. The doors were locked and there was no way out. Suddenly, they were all crawling towards me like spiders running across a web. I had nowhere to go. Suddenly, they all stopped. I heard a loud bang. It sounded like glass breaking. Before I could turn around, someone or something grabbed me. They pulled me through the window, cutting my back on the sharp glass. The zombies were following me through the window. I could smell the infection on them. I had to leave, I had to run...

Kacey Paige Jenkins (15)
Llanishen High School, Llanishen

Should I?

The fourth of July. Independence Day. The day I escaped with my life, on the edge of the infamous prison Alcatraz. I wound up here after being framed by our president himself, so it was up to me. Revenge was mine! I grabbed my secret gun stash and ran for my life. I knew I could make it, my friend was waiting for me. Then we struck. I had made it so far, should I pull the trigger? No, I should not. The temptation was too much. My legs trembled. It was the moment I'd waited for all my life!

Charlie Drysdale (12)

Llanishen High School, Llanishen

Hunted

I was running in the forest. My legs were on fire. I was tired. I had been running for ages. I fell on both of my legs, they were cut from my knees down to my shins. Someone was following me but I fell again, so I had to hide. I could hear the leaves crunching, second by second. Suddenly, there was no noise. I stood up but I heard breathing. I looked behind me, there he was. He raised his sharp knife. I heard a gunshot. *Bang!* There was my friend. The murderer dropped slowly down dead!

Daniel Mackay (12)
Llanishen High School, Llanishen

Innocent

The sirens wailed as I fell to the foot of my roommate's bed. The door burst open and I was being pulled away. I was in a state of panic and desperation, and I struggled to free myself before jumping out of the window of the Atlantic College dormitory. I ran until my legs ached and my throat burned, but I could still hear them on my tail. I dived behind a dumpster in an alleyway I had stumbled into and collapsed. I fell into hysterics as I saw them pass me. I didn't do it. I didn't kill her...

Amelia Nesbitt-Pearce (14)
Llanishen High School, Llanishen

The Chase

My pedal was pushed to the floor. I glided past cars on the dark open motorway. With sirens screeching, I couldn't stop now. Helicopters and cars trailed behind me like a cheetah chasing his prey. I was getting low on gas and beginning to panic. It felt like a game you would play on the PlayStation. It wasn't a matter of if I could escape, it was a matter of how long I could carry on for. A light appeared in my mirrors. They were close to me. My car began to slow. I was in trouble. Game over.

Henry Parker (12)
Llanishen High School, Llanishen

Run For Your Life!

We had to leave. Now. Knowing there was a murderer in the building my heart was racing so hard it could come up my throat. Suddenly all the lights turned off, so I ran. I kept running until I couldn't run anymore. I saw the fire doors and I went outside into the freezing cold, my feet were sinking into the snow. It's been a while since I stopped moving, there was nowhere to sleep. I saw the end to the woods and saw a lake that was frozen. I could see a figure in the distance staring at me...

Millie Exintaris (12)
Llanishen High School, Llanishen

24 Hours

We had twenty-four hours to find the ghost. We were very scared because the ghost was powerful. We were trying to hunt the ghost with my friends. We went into a room, it was filled with blood. We just wanted to leave the house, because one of my friends was screaming. We ran to where she was. She saw a person on the ground, blood everywhere. It was very dark, we could not see anything. We tried to find the ghost, we were hunting and hunting but then the wardrobe was moving. I just ran out.

Jasmeet Kaur (11)
Llanishen High School, Llanishen

The Hunt For George Kays

The sirens wailed. Shaking violently, I gripped my trousers. I could hear my own heart beating. I choked back the lump forming in my throat. I felt petrified. I could hear their footsteps on top of the log I was hiding in. I had just escaped from a research lab in Ohio. I had been on the run for twenty-four hours and couldn't run for much longer. I could see a torch beam aimed at a tree. A foot appeared at the end of the log. I made a break for it. I slipped under the fence. I was free...

Joshua Payne (12)
Llanishen High School, Llanishen

Red And Blue Lights

The sirens wailed in the distance as I ran from the silhouette of my shadow. Blue and red lights followed me across the city that was like a maze with no end. Chopping and turning around the corners that led to new streets that looked the same as the last. Trying to lose my silhouette in the red and blue lights. Never before have I had the feeling of being hunted, it sickened me. I couldn't run much longer, I took a turning that I regret to this very day. A dead end that changed me...

Harrison James (15)
Llanishen High School, Llanishen

Hunted

I had to swim away rapidly so the Mafia could not reach me. They were all very muscular. As I drifted away from the grand yacht, my friend Ryan started to panic. Suddenly, he got shot in the back with a rifle and sank like the Titanic. When I got to shore, I went to find my family, my wife, daughter and son. But first, I had to find them. I didn't know where they were. They could have been anywhere. I saw some police down at the bottom of the street so I asked them for help. At last!

James Daniel Wilson (12)
Llanishen High School, Llanishen

All Men's Nightmare

The sirens wailed as I hopped out of the dilapidated car and leapt into the forest, feeling scared, confused and worn out. I ran until I couldn't run any more. And that was when I saw it... My body froze and my heart shot out into the moonlight. I thought I was the hunter until I saw this beast of a man. A werewolf. I became the prey as it ran towards me. I ran faster than Usain Bolt through the forest until I tripped over a rock. I tried to get up but couldn't. I thought I was doomed...

Evan Heard (11)
Llanishen High School, Llanishen

Rats

The day had come upon us when we would go over. Half of the division was ill, and the other half was no longer with us. There was a bowl of cold soup next to me, but no one felt like eating. A rat scurried over a man's boot and lapped at his bowl, but he didn't seem to care.

"Two minutes, boys," a voice grunted. No one responded. If it was two minutes, it felt like two seconds. I heard a whistle blow in the distance and heard it get louder. I climbed out of the trench and ran...

Gabriel Franks (15)

Llanishen High School, Llanishen

The Virus

The sirens wailed as I ran through the forest but my Tourettes kicked in as my ankle twisted. I shouted, "Help!" as I faceplanted the dirt. I pushed myself up and turned my head to see a flashlight shining on me, into my eyes. He hit me over the head with a hydro-flask. I woke up to him standing right in front of me. "What did you do to me?" I tried to get up but I realised I was chained. I turned my head to see a half-empty syringe with green inside. He injected it into me. Sleep...

Daynton Jones (12)
Llanishen High School, Llanishen

I Escaped!

The sirens wailed as I escaped the cell. Guns blazing as I ran for my life, past the guards and out of the big black door. My legs burned and my feet were in agony. I was out of prison. I came into the field filled with oak trees and picnic benches. I suddenly heard a branch snap behind me. I turned and saw the guard standing there with his big dark blue shotgun. He grabbed me by the neck and dragged me all the way back to my small prison cell. Until next time. I will escape again...

Abbie Cruse (15)
Llanishen High School, Llanishen

The Mask

I stood there, all I could hear was howling. Maybe the forest was haunted. Ten years ago there were hunters roaming these exact forests but they never ever came out. Nobody knows what had happened to them. I kept seeing things like masks, I wasn't sure if it was just in my head. I saw it again. I was definitely not imagining it. I had a feeling there was something on my back, like a hand. I turned behind me and saw a mask, and ran as far as I could from the mask, out of the forest...

Mollie Westerman (12)
Llanishen High School, Llanishen

The Race

All I could do was stand there and stare at it. When suddenly I found myself running towards it, my heart pounded faster and faster. The smell drifted towards me, it smelt like freedom! As I started to get closer my opponent caught up and we were neck and neck. He tried to distract me but I resisted and kept my eye on the prize; the end was near. In the last few seconds, it felt fantastic as I had managed to gain the lead. I had won the last chocolate bar in the house! Pure delight!

Emma Brotherton (11)
Llanishen High School, Llanishen

The Escape

I had twenty-four hours to escape my room. My heart was pounding. It was beating as fast as a cheetah chasing after its prey. When my parents were busy watching a film on the sofa I snuck downstairs to get some food and met up with my friend down the street to hide away from my parents, who had hunted me down my entire life. I hid and hid until I could not hide any more. I was so tired, so thirsty, so hungry. I wonder if they'll ever find me and if I'll ever see them again?

Shannon Lynch (13)
Llanishen High School, Llanishen

Hunted

It's not safe now they know. I had just been trying to get supplies when it saw me. The Assault Bot had been hunting me ever since I blew up Parliament. The out of control robot has been killing people left right and centre. Looking for its target. Me. I need help right now. I was not the only one there so why was it looking for me? I heard a loud bang. It had found me! I ran through the fire exit to the roof. The blood on the Bot was a deep crimson. What was going to happen?

Alfie Sell (12)
Llanishen High School, Llanishen

The Spotlight

A bright flash hit me from above. It was a circular shape. I started pacing out of the woods but every time I looked up, it was there. This time I ran faster than I ever did before but all of a sudden I froze. I couldn't move a muscle. I was terrified that I would never see my family ever again. Unexpectedly, I was levitating. It was like the circular thing was sucking me in. I was inside. There were weird objects and I started hearing things in a whole different language...

Fabio Correia (11)
Llanishen High School, Llanishen

Run

I was running. I didn't know where, but I was running, trying to just get away. I could hear the loud thudding of their boots behind me. I felt faint. I couldn't run, but I had to. I had to get away. I turned a sharp corner, hoping they would lose me. It turned out to be a dead end. This maze was a trick. There was no escape. I heard a gunshot. It sounded close. Like it was right behind me. A sharp pain hit my head. Blood was everywhere. My blood. There was no escape from death.

Rhianna Hayes (13)
Llanishen High School, Llanishen

Hunter Becomes Hunted

I had twenty-four hours. The girl with a red hood hunted me, as I'd hunted her for three weeks. I had to ice her today, or I'd be the dead one. She was in the forest with a bag of goods heading towards her grandma's home. I had to get there before her. I crept in through the back door. I saw the grandma, ate the grandma. I dressed up as her just as the girl walked in. Her knife was big. She was hunting me. I knew I had to leave right then. I was now being hunted...

Dylan John Clarke (13)
Llanishen High School, Llanishen

Deep Dark Hole

I ran to a deep dark place from the person who was chasing me. I began to panic, the siren wailed looking for me. I went down a deep hole, my legs ached, my legs had holes in them. I was waiting for my death. I heard wolves howling, leaves rustling, all I could say was, "Wow." He found me. I had to climb back up and run for my life. Oh my god, he was behind me. Time to run. I sprinted with fear. I sprinted past a road, when everything stopped, even me. But not him...

Will Lewis (14)

Llanishen High School, Llanishen

The Disaster

I had twenty-four hours. I had to build a base. My family and I got plenty of metal and started burrowing. It was finished. All we needed was food. Once we were back, we had one hour left. My arms stung, my legs felt like they were being stabbed. We were done with five minutes to spare. We hopped in the bunker and hoped it would hold. We were in the bunker for ten minutes and nothing happened. All of a sudden, we heard a bang. Was it the water? Would we survive? Would we die?

Cieran Joshua Williams (12)
Llanishen High School, Llanishen

Eleven

Where can I hide? I couldn't run for much longer. I'd become the prey. It's not safe now they know what I am. I had escaped from the facility. Luckily I saw something up ahead, my throat hurting like there were pins in it, I was close to the hut, it might be a place to eat, so I ran as fast as I could. In broad daylight, it was hard to escape. I went in through the back door and it was a kitchen. I saw chips on the counter when suddenly the sirens started. I ran to escape...

Ricardo Moreira (12)
Llanishen High School, Llanishen

Trapped

The sound of silence has never felt so loud. If I just make a run for it, I'll be out, free. No. Of course, I can't. It's too risky. She's calling my name, her frail voice beginning to close in on me. I can feel my heartbeat in every inch of my body. I need to get out of here. I haven't got long left. I stand up, the not-so-subtle creaking of the floorboards beneath me, sending shivers up my spine. There's every chance she heard me. This is it. Running, I figure it's over...

Lois Taylor (15)
Llanishen High School, Llanishen

Mistaken In Jail...

I sprinted as the police chased me. I couldn't run for much longer, I was exhausted. I had no clue why they were chasing me, but there was no time to check about that. I saw posters of an imposter disguised as me; I wanted to tell the police. As the sirens wailed, I tripped over, looking up to a police officer... I was thrown in jail, telling them I was innocent. Obviously they couldn't be convinced since I had no evidence. How could I certify that I am innocent?

Ibrahim Shvan Saadallah (11)
Llanishen High School, Llanishen

Hunted

I screamed. Nothing. I screamed again, even though it was hard to do. I was struggling to get up from where I was lying but some type of force was holding me back. Unexpectedly, a hand came out of nowhere and something bit me. I was in excruciating pain. I realised that it is somewhat obvious that I was going to die any minute. A tear rolled down my cheek, then lots more came down as I thought about my husband, that I can't talk to anymore, and my beloved children...

Sian Isabel Darnell (11)
Llanishen High School, Llanishen

The Chase

A scream! A screech! A silence! It was my fault. Why did I do this? To be rich? To be tough? Why? This is going to be the end of me! Should I run? Or should I just stay and get caught? No. I can do this. I'm going to get out and run. I'm running. Running for my life. Running for me. I hear sirens wailing behind me, Getting louder and louder, with every step I take. Every breath I breathe. I run and run. I stop. And stood glaring at me is a police officer. Waiting for me.

Millie Tran (11)
Llanishen High School, Llanishen

Broken

Twenty-four hours... I was trapped in a small dark wood. The leaves had no trees or the trees had no leaves... I don't know? Everything was spinning, my head, my brain, and maybe the world? All I knew was this was not a utopia. I was about to run, but suddenly a long, tall, thin man with no face looked down on me! I was paralysed. Frozen still. His face started to crack like an ugly person in a mirror. I knew I was about to be hunted, and I knew who my hunter was...

Mya Gascoyne (13)
Llanishen High School, Llanishen

Hunted!

Once there was a boy who had three problems. One, he lived by a haunted house. Two, he didn't know who lived there. Three, he didn't know if he could go in or not. He said to himself, "I'm going in there to see what is going on!" As he walked up the path he saw the lights switch on and then the car lights. He stopped for a second and said, "I'm only dreaming." As he got to the front door, it opened like someone was there. The open door was waiting for him. But he ran.

Owain Andrews (11)

Llanishen High School, Llanishen

Hunted

I had twenty-four hours. I didn't know where I was but all I knew was I had to run. I ran through the woods as quick as I could. *Bang!* I faceplanted the floor. I got up and realised I fell over a six-foot-long log. I kept running until I got to a cave. I decided to go to sleep for an hour or two. I fell asleep straight away. I heard someone outside step on a twig. I thought I was sleeping but I realised this was real. Time was up. I was now being hunted!

Riley Breadmore (12)
Llanishen High School, Llanishen

Hunted

My legs were trembling as I was breaking out of jail. The sirens went off, they sounded like a shop alarm, and the police were looking for me. I had to get out if it was the last thing I ever did. I knew I should not have been put in jail in the first place, so I was angry at the police. I got out, it was hard, but I was out and running. There were police cars and helicopters all looking for me. I didn't know where I was running to. Then a police car hit me...

Daniel Jenkins
Llanishen High School, Llanishen

The Ghost

Today my life changed forever. I was on the run. I ran for as long as I could until I hit the cold wet floor. There I was, aching in pain, my torso aching and my legs burning like someone stuck a knife through them. I could hear them getting closer. At this moment, I could see flashes and hear sirens coming towards me. I lifted my face up in pain, I stumbled and tried to run. From the corner of my eye, I could see my best friend. I ran to her as fast as I could...

Molly Mermaid Mary Tina Patsy Kavanagh (12)
Llanishen High School, Llanishen

The Chase

The bright blue night sky looked upon me with a blue moon. Lighting hit as the clock struck twelve, and Barry and I started to deform into wolves. We had to scuttle away as fast as possible, but a police officer had seen us and caught us on video. Out of nowhere a SWAT team appeared and cornered us. One of the members looked into my eyes. My eyes turned red, and I grew to the size of a bear. By then, nothing could affect me. Barry and I escaped to the hide-out...

Jakub Otrusina (13)
Llanishen High School, Llanishen

Running For My Life

Running for my life, nowhere to go. I've been running for hours but it feels like days. I know they are going to find me and take me back but by the time they get here, I'll be gone. I'll make sure they won't find me, no one will. All of a sudden I see lights in the distance. I know they can see me. Panicking, I begin to run, my body in pain. It's a dead-end, I'm by a cliff. What, no, I shouldn't... What will I do? Should I jump? Run? Hide? I don't know...

Maddie McNamee (12)
Llanishen High School, Llanishen

The Hunt

I had twenty-four hours to get money from the bank. We were within touching distance. My legs swung as fast as they could but I couldn't run for much longer. I got to the bank before it closed. I snuck in, grabbed all the treasure and ran, but all of a sudden I heard the siren wail really loudly. I climbed up on the roof and ran down the other side as fast as I could and sprinted away. I got home. Huh, I'm as brave as a tiger! Never, ever again...

Mason Aaron Cornock (12)
Llanishen High School, Llanishen

Hunted

It was a stormy, windy day as I drove down the eerie lane. Every mile I drove, it was getting gloomier and gloomier. As time passed I soon sensed a presence in the back seat of my car. As I went to check, a big man with a black cloak hooked me around my neck. I struggled as much as I could but it was no use! He left me alone to grab something from his car and I seized my chance and got away. Not for long though, the thing he got from his car was a gun!

Coel Sigerson
Llanishen High School, Llanishen

When They Whirled Through My Veins!

The gases filled the atmosphere like a stinkbomb, rapidly diffusing.

"Run for your life!" The pressure was building up inside me, about to combust. It halted me dead in my tracks! I spluttered, stumbled, merely managing to shift a step. The poison whirled through my veins, killing every slither of life left in me. Other soldiers pelted on, but the gases wouldn't pause. As I lay in excruciating pain I pondered... will we ever win?! It had fully taken over as I lay to rest in peace. My allies were far from peace though, they must persevere in this war!

Claudia Sefton (11)
Malvern St James Girls' School, Great Malvern

Hunted

"It's not safe. They know," I said, keeping my voice down.
"Ssh, they'll hear you! It has to be here somewhere, " said
Savannah as she searched. We had been out there for hours
trying to find the necklace. As the sun crept upon us, we had
very little time.

"Find it or else," is what we keep hearing in our heads; the
croaky voice of the man. Hearing that phrase keep popping
up in our heads made us ache for that necklace. We never
understood what was so special about it, but we
remembered what the man said...

Panda Lacey (11)
Malvern St James Girls' School, Great Malvern

The Hunt

Loud noises were coming from all around me. A circle of sound surrounding the meadow, trapping my senses, trapping me. Strange roars were coming closer and closer. *Bang!* A loud shot rang out clearly through the air. What was going on? Other hares near me were running about in the confusion. I couldn't focus clearly. A pheasant lay, injured on the ground. What had done this? I saw a large two-legged figure. It had three arms. One was made of steel, shooting metal bullets. The game season had begun. We were hares, and we were being hunted.

Bessy Baxter (12)
Malvern St James Girls' School, Great Malvern

The Game

"We have to go," I shouted. They said it was like a game of hide-and-seek but no, it was much worse. Everyone was running and screaming. It was too distressing, so I just ran, until I heard a horrific scream. It was my best friend, he'd been turned. I found a place to keep safe, it was all going great apart from the devilish screams, but then sirens started blaring in my ears. I knew it was too late. It meant they'd started releasing a virus that would kill us all. Then everything stopped. The only thing there was... nothingness.

Phoebe Tabitha Trevelyan (11)
Malvern St James Girls' School, Great Malvern

Every Year

Every year. Every single year. And out of how many? Seven billion? How was I chosen? And... I... didn't know they would wipe my memory, leaving only the rules of the tournament. They've left me with nothing. They just dropped me here, to my certain death. No. Not just me. Others. Ten other children. I wonder how many will make the night. I hold my breath as the countdown begins. Five... four... three... two... one... and I'm out of time. I sprint as fast as I can from the others. If they can't catch me, they can't kill me...

Imogen Carys Hayes (12)
Malvern St James Girls' School, Great Malvern

Where Am I?

"We have to leave. Now." Those were my last words. Now I don't know where I am. All I see is shadowy black, slowly creeping into me like poison. We were being hunted, I think. It's so hard to remember now. But I think, I think I died. I remember what was hunting us though. Some called them angels, but we called them demons. They were indestructible and invulnerable. Many people fell to them. Those that lived I doubt I'll ever see again. I doubt I'll ever know what they were. But now, I want to know where I am.

Amber McAndrew (11)

Malvern St James Girls' School, Great Malvern

The Fear

It was a very happy time until they came. The happiness of playing hide-and-seek. The joyfulness was diffusing everywhere around me. It was dark, it's a full moon tonight. I had to go home. On the way home the lights were flickering, but only when I walked past. Fear slowly filled me from the end of my toe to the top of my head. An icy wind blew, but it was very hot in my heart. There was no light any more, pitch-black was in front of me!
"Why didn't you go home, little girl? Now you're definitely mine!"

Xuan Xia (11)
Malvern St James Girls' School, Great Malvern

Hunted

I was walking through the woods when I heard something behind me. I wasn't sure what it was, so I started running quicker and quicker. Whatever was behind me didn't stop, it got closer and closer. That's when I realised, I was being hunted. A few minutes later, I saw a tree. It looked easy to climb, I thought, so I climbed it. It soon got dark. Suddenly, I fell out of the tree.

"Ouch!" I yelled. Just then, the creature appeared that had been chasing me. I realised that it was a baby cheetah!

Evangeline Maya Ede (11)
Malvern St James Girls' School, Great Malvern

Busted

Oh, no. They're bound to find out what I've done. No. Surely they won't know, right? I'm standing there, looking as if Medusa had stared directly at me. I look to my left, red and blue lights flash so rapidly I almost forget I'm in the middle of an open road. I have to make a decision. Quick, quick, think! I run, no I *bolt*. I lose my breath but definitely don't stop. Leaving the lifeless bleeding body behind, my two legs drag me along. Three tall terrifying shadows. I gasp and drop my knife. Busted.

April-Louise Sadler (11)
Malvern St James Girls' School, Great Malvern

The Easter Hunt

Ding, dong. The doorbell rang, my friends have come over for an Easter egg hunt. They all came running in and we played some games, I looked out of the window and saw a fluffy creature, I was so shocked. Could it be the Easter bunny? I told my friends and ran outside. I saw loads of Easter eggs, they were in trees, in bushes, in flowers. I looked around and saw two big long ears. I tried to chase the creature and I found eggs buried behind it. Finally, I saw what it really was - the Easter bunny!

Elizabeth Chloe Motteram (12)
Malvern St James Girls' School, Great Malvern

Hide-And-Seek

It was like a dangerous game of hide-and-seek. First, they're right in front of you, but then, they're gone again. I've had many experiences, but none like this. I was set a mission. I let my gun shoot, but I missed. He ran. As fast as he could. I couldn't keep up. I chased him, but I was too slow. He was gone, just like that. My friends told me not to worry about it. But what did they know? They weren't spies like me. Or were they? And that's just it. I would never know, would I?

Ceri Smith (12)
Malvern St James Girls' School, Great Malvern

The Disease

It was bright red, oozing a thick yellow substance. It was as if a tennis ball was growing under my skin. My arm was in extreme pain, the weight of the lump was dragging my arm down. The doctors said they would need to amputate in the next twenty-four hours, or my whole arm would fall off, killing me slowly and extremely painfully. The problem was that they had amputated hundreds of lumps and had no anaesthetic left. It would hurt, but not as much as if they left it. So I had no choice but to amputate...

Freya Wall (11)
Malvern St James Girls' School, Great Malvern

Diseased

The sirens wailed, I put on my vaccination suit and rushed out. I could see them running towards us, banging on the gates. I got my weapons straight away and started killing them as fast and as many as I could, but there were just so many. I watched my fellow soldiers being torn apart by these diseased creatures, they were ripping out brains and hearts... but I knew we had to keep going. My best friend got shot down and the beasts could smell the blood wafting through the air. Then it happened... Noooo!

Ilana Coldicott (11)
Malvern St James Girls' School, Great Malvern

A Horrid Dream

Thirty minutes, twenty-nine minutes, twenty-eight minutes... I must get out of here, or else I won't see my family and friends again. I won't get to go to the places I want to ever again. My heartbeat is fast, I feel like eyes are looking at me. I feel like ghosts are chasing after me. I hope that a prince will save me, but this is not a fairy tale. I think hard, which way shall I go, north, south, east, or west? I have no compass, no more food. No! Suddenly an alarm rang. Oh, it was my alarm...

Ella Chan (11)
Malvern St James Girls' School, Great Malvern

The Attack

My face was as pale as a ghost. I looked around, they were just staring at me like they had been abducted. My heart was pounding. I didn't know where to look. One of them gave me a dirty look, scrunching their nose, another one looked me up and down, looking at my neon yellow jumper like it was something stupid or ugly. They all started to move and make a path for someone special. I held my breath and crossed my toes. Then one of them walked through and beckoned me.
"Goo goo gaga!"

Islay Allen (11)
Malvern St James Girls' School, Great Malvern

Hunted

There they were. I couldn't hide for much longer. I knew it, they were going to find me. My eyes closed as the tension built up and up and up, until, "No, no, no!" I yelled as they approached me. "Help!" I screamed. "Aargh! Aargh! Get off!" I mumbled as they got under the duvet. I opened my eyes gently to the sight of fearsome jaws surrounding my view. What were they going to do? Suddenly police swung my door open and rescued me! I slept soundly that night, well... at least until... *bang!*

Imogen Hobbs (11)
Malvern St James Girls' School, Great Malvern

The Escape Was On!

I was out, out of the filthy prison. Freedom was mine. I could hear sirens wailing in my ears. The hunt was on. I had to move quickly if I wanted to survive. I could hear sirens gaining on me. They were getting closer and closer. My legs were aching, I couldn't run for much longer. I was on my own in the middle of the night, in the middle of nowhere. I turned sharply down a narrow alleyway and found myself cornered. There were police at the end and police at the start. Oh, blast! I was busted!

Elizabeth Rose Sylvia Bryant (11)

Malvern St James Girls' School, Great Malvern

The Perfect Dress

Blood-curdling screams echoed around the shop. I could see concerned faces turn to face me but I didn't care, all I could think about was getting this dress, my dress! It was soon going to be my wedding and I had found the perfect dress. As soon as I saw it I knew I had to get it. But it wasn't only me who wanted it. Someone elbowed me in the ribs, I could feel a bruise starting to form. It was war! I grabbed the dress and ran. I could hear screaming women behind me. I was being chased...

Natalia Rolinson (11)
Malvern St James Girls' School, Great Malvern

The Chase

I was running. I had no idea how long I'd been running for. It felt like hours, it was probably only a few minutes. I don't even know if it was still there. Was it after me? It was like a wild beast. I turned my head to see if it was there. The last thing I remember was feeling myself fall. Falling down, down, down until I felt a rush of cold and my body being pushed somewhere. I didn't know. I was whacked in the face by a freezing liquid. I went under and passed out.

Bethany Williams (12)
Malvern St James Girls' School, Great Malvern

The Breakout!

My friends and I have been planning our escape for years. We have slowly been digging a tunnel. An escape tunnel. It leads out through the sewers into the main city. We are leaving tomorrow. We have saved bread and biscuits, clothes and toiletries. Anything we might need, we have got it. All we need now is no lockdowns or guards to find out our plan! If this all works out, then we will be free to walk out into the world...

Madeleine Mary Beckett (12)
Malvern St James Girls' School, Great Malvern

The Game Of Terror

Traumatised, I hide. My heart practically dancing out of my chest.

"Ready or not, here I come!" A child's worst nightmare. Those deathly words like ice down my neck. I hear him thumping up the stairs. My mind panicking. One thought drowning out the others - *don't get caught!* I am trying to breathe quietly, but my breath just wants to jump out of my body and scream.

"Where are you?" No! He's coming closer! I can hear him. He's here. "I know you're in here!" Before I know it the door swings open; I wish we didn't play hide-and-seek...

Mia Getty (11)

Rosebery School, Epsom

The Unpredictable

At first, it looked like a ship rising over the horizon, so commonplace that it slipped straight through my vision. But people didn't scream about ships, or see one on the horizon and abandon their possessions, strewn about the beach, to run inland for their lives. People picked up everything from children to dogs to beachballs and tore away from the beach in a panicked crowd. The earlier sunshine was dimming by the minute.The higher the waves rose, the lower the hopes plunged of the terrified people, streaking through the town, running with one communal aim: staying alive.

Holly Hughes-Ehrke (12)
Rosebery School, Epsom

Runaway Slave

I had to escape. Their cruelty and inhumanity struck me, and I just had to run, the treacherous ground beneath my bruised, blistered feet. My head was uncontrollably fuzzy, and my heart was frantically pounding against my chest like a drum. *Thump, thump,* my heart went. Pathetic tears drizzled down my scarred face, I had to keep going, to escape the devils. Being a slave isn't easy, in fact, it's brutal and appallingly dreadful. Powerfully, they would whip and slap me, they treated me as if I was as little and useless as an ant. I had to go...

Rosie Joyce (13)
Rosebery School, Epsom

Ready Or Not

My bruised legs felt like jelly; my swollen heart was thumping out of my scarred chest, and I could feel eyes burning into my shattered soul. I wasn't alone. Someone was here. Shakily, I turned around, expecting to be faced with a strange silhouette, but nothing. The longer I stood, the deeper I felt the menacing pair of eyes sinking into me. Without thinking, I dropped down, embracing the feel of the sticky mud on my bony face. Silently, tears escaped my eyes and slid down my now moist face. That feeling again. I looked up only to discover him...

Mia Cole (12)
Rosebery School, Epsom

The Man On The Moon...

I have twenty-four hours. Twenty-four hours to run, hide and escape the clutches of the man on the moon. Once again, he will snatch an innocent child, plunging them into his fortress on the dark side of the moon. Parents stowaway their children, however, us orphans have to fend for ourselves, darting through the woods, praying that he will steal a different child. Panicking, I trip over a stone and taste the bitter blood in my mouth. I scramble to my feet, my time is up. I can already see his shadowy figure looking before me. I have been chosen...

Eliza Mae Wormley (12)
Rosebery School, Epsom

Running

Meg was running; running for her life. The planes were swooping in like birds catching their prey, bombs dropping to the ground, chasing her. She was only thirteen; too young to have to flee from her house in the night, leaving her family to die. Where the ocean was, there were plenty of hiding places, but being on top of a cliff wasn't helpful. The alliance was hunting down every citizen and didn't care how you died, as long as you were dead. Now Meg was faced with a cliff. She jumped, knowing her fate wasn't going to be pretty...

Jas Rae Pelton (12)
Rosebery School, Epsom

Mortis

I ran, but death is not something you can run from... I first saw her at Trafalgar Square. My family has been known for many different things, and by many different names, but right now mine is Calliope Angelus Mortis, or Calliope, Angel of Death. Seeing who was haunting me at the time, the name seemed fitting - looking back it seems a mockery. I first saw Mortis, or Death, by Trafalgar Square but it wasn't the first time I suspected she had been watching. She has been watching my family for decades but has never acted, until now...

Eleanor Baldwin (13)
Rosebery School, Epsom

Use Your Differences

I ran as fast as I could, barely catching my breath. I could hear them behind me, they were close. Why did I have to be so different? I hastily sped up to the lake, left or right? I contemplated the reason they were after me. I had an idea... I could use the reason as an advantage, so I did! I jumped into the lake and swam under the water. Would they know? Soon after, my legs disappeared and turned into a shiny gold tail. I was a mermaid. I swam away. I was safe for now.

Ellah Milner (11)
Rosebery School, Epsom

Desert Ancients

It was so close. The speeding triceratops needed to relocate, away from its relentless predators - the velociraptors. Across the burning sands of its desert habitat, the quadruped dashed at lightning speed, but its pursuers were even faster, catching it up, getting ever closer, until... *slash!* The deadly raptors clawed at their prey, scratching and swiping at every cell of its being. The triceratops jabbed at them with its horned face and swiped at them with its long tail. With the predators floored, the triceratops made its bid for freedom. But the deadly raptors would strike back - for vengeance!

Alexander David Taylor (13)

Spalding Grammar School, Spalding

Go Down Fighting

Sirens wailed all around me. Some incoherent jumble poured out of a hidden megaphone. I made out the words, "You are completely surrounded." I took off, my heart pounding in my chest. I ran into an old warehouse and locked and bolted the door. Suddenly, the door started to shake. From outside a voice yelled, "We know you're in there!" I hid behind some packaging crates as the door burst open. Silhouettes slipped into the room, brandishing weapons.

I felt the outline of the gun in my pocket. I gripped it tightly, reassuring myself.

I planned to go down fighting.

Ryan Ream (13)

Spalding Grammar School, Spalding

The Marksman

The death rattle of machine guns was deafening, the staccato of rifle fire echoed across the battlefield. Whistling shells screamed over, slamming into the ground in flashes of white fire. Screams and cries came close to drowning out the titanic roar of explosions. I crouched down in the mud, bloodstained hands shaking like the ground beneath my feet. I raised the rifle. Aimed. Fired. Slaughtered. I was thrown to the ground in a whirling vortex, the rifle wrenched from my grasp, the ground ripped apart, blood running down my face. At last, my hunt was over. Keep going, friends...

Isaac Roes (10)
Spalding Grammar School, Spalding

The Copse

We were close. We knew they were there, down in the copse. They had been there for over twelve hours. We had been there since they ambushed our recce patrol. There were twelve of us: ten with L98GP rifles, two with light support weapons. I saw the glint of gunmetal coming from the copse. As I pressed safety onto fire and pulled the trigger, nine other rifles echoed before the support weapons roared into action, decimating the tree line, not even giving them time to react. As the gunfire stopped, we advanced. I saw him too late. He opened fire.

Archie Morant (13)
Spalding Grammar School, Spalding

The Metal Bloodhounds

The sirens wailed like an injured dog, as the police cars sniffed me out as if they were great metal bloodhounds. The blue lights cast their colour across the walls beside me. Cold puddle water splashed up my trousers. Why had I stolen it? It wasn't worth it. As I ran, I contemplated throwing it away, denying all affiliation with it. It was then that I made my mistake. I rounded the corner and entered a dead-end alleyway. I backed up against the wall. My heart pounding. The police car pulled up. They found me. Time to accept my fate...

Mark Edwards (12)
Spalding Grammar School, Spalding

Hunted

A cold lash of wind catches my cheek as I race away through this decrepit forest. The eyes follow me, with ground-shattering footsteps trailing my every move. All I can do is run. Keep going into this seemingly endless abyss. I can't help but look back, only to notice that it's faster now, gaining on me quickly. I hear the sounds of the demonic beast, taking turns to escape its wretched form. Nothing is working. Is this the end? Am I going to die? Why am I being hunted like some weak feeble animal?

Connor Batch (15)

Spalding Grammar School, Spalding

He Brought His Knife Upon Me

I stopped suddenly. My heart was racing like a formula one car. I looked behind me fearfully as I caught my breath. My eyes darted wildly as I looked for the man. I could imagine the man sniffing me out. I felt like prey as my predator tried to find me. Suddenly, my fears came true, I saw the man walking menacingly towards me. His malevolent grin was enough to scare anyone. His knife glistened in the moonlight as he charged at me. I stood rooted to the ground in fear as he bought his knife upon me...

Vedant Gadkari (13)
Spalding Grammar School, Spalding

Ribbet

I ran. Just ran. My mind was blank. I was moving my legs, pumping my arms, leaping over rotting logs. I could hear them behind me, gaining on me. I was too scared to turn back. I tripped on a rock jutting from the ground. I turned and saw... nothing. Where were they? Then I heard it. "Come on, you know you want to!" It said. "Join us!" I stumbled up and ran. As I did so, something small landed on my back. It leapt like nothing should. It sank its fangs into my neck. The vampire frogs had won!

Ben Hales (12)
Spalding Grammar School, Spalding

The Alien

Then I saw him, his eyes as black as coal. My leather shoes are worn, and my legs leaden and filled with pain. I then stumbled. Darkness crept over me like spiders on my back. I cannot get up. I cannot breathe. I cannot move, whilst his ebony tentacles wrapped around my neck. Like a vulture circling its prey, death came. He celebrated his victory by pecking my corpse, like a ravenous bird. Finally, he had accomplished his mission. Disappearing, he turned into dust, never to be seen again...

Matthew William Cobb (11)

Spalding Grammar School, Spalding

Corridors

I have three minutes to get out of these endless corridors. The lights flicker and dim as I run. The musty air brushes my face. The turning corridors make my head spin. I try to run but the creature has me in its mental grasp. My heart threatens to burst out of my chest. My legs ache but panic keeps me going. It smells my fear and it laughs. My legs stop moving. It's coming. I hear screams. My screams. It's here. Memories are lost as darkness closes in.

Gregory Pool (11)
Spalding Grammar School, Spalding

The Hunt

The sirens deafen me as I hop over the wall. I run as if my life depends on it, which it does. My tattered clothes rip on the barbed wire. I run into the dense woods and hear the clattering of boots. I hide behind a tree, I can see a lodge. A vehicle approaches. Agents are going to the door and telling her that a prisoner has escaped. He was jailed for stalking. I am that prisoner. The owner goes to bed. I move towards her. Her house. Her bedroom. Her.

Thien Clare (12)
Spalding Grammar School, Spalding

Robbery

I cannot stop. I hear the sirens wailing, the lights surrounding me. I run, my back is dead - sprinting with a few kilograms on your back is not nice. Over a fence, into an alley. A few police units stop just outside. They run after me. They pour in from the other side too. I didn't want to do this, I thought. I pull out my gun and run, run, shooting the police - but with sleep darts. I do not intend to kill anyone. I've escaped, but what next...

Caspian Szczygiel (11)
Spalding Grammar School, Spalding

The Grand Escape

They'd found me. The airfield was near. I had to run. I was almost there. I hopped in a jet. No time to get to a runway, I put full throttle on and took off. I banked right and saw someone following me. *Boom!* I heard an explosion to my right. *Boom!* Then to my left. My left aileron was down. I was spinning randomly. I closed my eyes and hoped for the best. Will I ever open them again?

Ben Booth (12)
Spalding Grammar School, Spalding

Pretty Little Treat

Crimson-red. Her smell, her scent, it stains my mind crimson-red, forcing a haze over my restless eyes. Factory fumes thicken my throat, pollute my tongue, but I continue. One foot forward, then the other, down labyrinth streets, navigating a concrete maze. Her life-blood calls to me, begs me to hurry. I do. A jog, a run, through dismal alley after dismal alley; she can't hide. There! Tentative murmurs, a delicate heartbeat, drumming softly. Another desolate corner, crumbling brick giving way to my fingertips as I lurch forwards - sweet parted lips, honey eyes, exposed neck. Delicious.
"Good evening, darling..."

Oskar Leonard (16)
St John Rigby College, Orrell

Bloody Laundry

So this was how my action film-worthy backstory started. Lone-wolf girl in apocalyptic world vows to seek revenge and hunt down the undead that killed her family. Pfft! More like, terrified teenager winds up in a ramshackle laundromat in Brixton, a horde of the infected on her tail. Before 'they' had taken over, life had been quietly perfect. Now, they were hammering against the fractured glass windows, moaning for their next meal... me. As the door shattered, unleashing the undead monsters, I knew then that my backstory was actually my ending. Who knew that the hunter could become the hunted...

Holly Fairhurst (17)

St John Rigby College, Orrell

Jack

Waiting in the cobbled alleyway, I adjusted my hat, swept down my coat, and waited patiently in the encroaching darkness... waiting for the next victim. I could hear their voices in the tavern, all of their laughing, crying, moaning... it made me sick to my stomach. Suddenly I heard the door swing open, a naive drunkard came stumbling down the tavern's stairs into my trap.

"Little harlot..." I muttered under my breath. The way my prey jostled and gasped as the sheer sound of my voice alone gave me much pleasure. Her death made me feel so alive...

Caner Aydin (16)
St John Rigby College, Orrell

Ambush

We had them where we wanted them, at the bottom of the valley. In a forest as dense as this, the only way to ensure a victory was getting to higher ground and knowing where the enemy is. Our scouts had seen a large group of theirs and told us the best way to surround them, we all got stealthily in position, and many of us had eyes on them. A signal passed between us and we waited silently for the last one before we charged. Then a twig snapped behind me. They had us where they wanted us...

Leah Jeffries (17)
St John Rigby College, Orrell

You're Mine

He was certain she was the one for him. His heart leapt at the sight of her, and her heart had never beaten so fast. At last, his long hunt for the love of his life was over. All he needed to do was convince her to feel the same. She knew about her secret admirer of course. She knew his gaze and how it made her hair stand on end. She recognised his heavy footsteps and struggled breath. She didn't know him but he knew her. Her scent was unique. Then she felt his hand on her shoulder...

Abigail Eve Donlon (17)
St John Rigby College, Orrell

The Flood

It was a cold, miserable day. I was at school when it happened. The bell rang and everyone hurried to go upstairs because the flood was rising. Everyone was panicked as they could see people and houses drowning in the furious flood. Some of my classmates were left outside and we were worried where our parents were. The tragedy only lasted for a minute, but the flood sent lots of death and destruction. The flood was gone! Children burst into tears when their parents didn't show up. I'm lucky because my mother is with me always. Luckily, she's my teacher!

Pheobe Dimdore (13)
Stewards Academy, Harlow

Danger In The Air

The crack of a twig, the rustling of leaves. I awaken from my slumber - there's danger in the air. I may be a fierce animal but I still feel fear. I emerge from my den. I hear heavy breathing. There's a loud bang and a warm feeling shoots through me. I go limp. I look around. Humans pull my mane. I lose consciousness. I awaken to unfamiliar surroundings. I'm encased in a clear substance. Small children stare at me. I roar to intimidate them. They seem amused by this. I settle down, accepting what has happened to me.

Edward Paul Austin (13)

Stewards Academy, Harlow

The Hunt Is On!

I heard sirens. I knew at that moment they were after me. I ran and ran until I couldn't run anymore. Wolves howled. Guns fired. I was the bunny, they were the wolves. Predator versus prey. My heart raced. In my head, all these thoughts flashed. What did I do wrong? How did this happen? I knew it wasn't safe anymore. I had to leave. *Run! For god's sake run*, I told myself. I heard voices. Someone said my name. I knew I was being hunted once and for all. Guns fired again. Oh no! They were too close. *Bang!*

Isabella Constable (11)

Stewards Academy, Harlow

The Lost Key

I had twenty-four hours to find the jewel-encrusted golden key. I could feel it tickling my fingers while holding a candlelit torch. This rare key had special healing powers that would make you live forever.

We were close. As I entered the damp cove, a smell of seaweed crashed into my face like a stink bomb. Another explorer was next to me.

"I saw a key in a chest next to a mine," he said.

I could run for much longer. I saw the mine and the chest. I opened the chest and there it was - the key!

Taylor Woolley (12)

Stewards Academy, Harlow

In Hiding!

My heavy head lay on the pillow as thousands of thoughts raced through my mind. Where am I going now? It was a restless night of being on the run. I wasn't safe, but I'd better get used to it. Little did I know, this was only the beginning. Long nights. Cold hands. It was getting hard to form my words. I was overwhelmed, tired, lost. Every night I'd wake up to tears trembling down my face onto my pillow and my body rocking side to side. It was charades; not knowing where to turn next.

Taygan Harris (12)
Stewards Academy, Harlow

Escape Room

He scrambled around the room, frantically poring over dozens of papers, books and globes. Strands of string connecting points on a map enveloped him in an avalanche of information, like some sort of crude spider's web. All he needed was a code, any code to escape from the horrible nightmare that awaited him if he was too slow. He watched the timer. Thirty seconds left. He pounded the wall with his fists in frustration, knowing that his inevitable death was waiting for him. He felt his own blood trickling through his fingers and closed his eyes, waiting for his demise.

Thomas Wang (14)
The Purcell School, Bushey

The Werewolf Transformation

Five minutes. The air was penetrating my flesh, the huntsman powering through, as if unaffected. Four minutes. The smell of humankind was a cross between white rose petals and the stench of onions; neither I found a pleasing scent. Three minutes. Nothing was more daunting than knowing that your kind's existence relied solely on your ability to bound through the grounds of the coppice. Two minutes. A creature like me should not feel fear as humans do. One minute. I sensed the toll of the bell for midnight. Three. Two. One. My werewolf form at last.

Jessica Christine Briany Hendry (14)
The Purcell School, Bushey

We Had Twenty-Four Hours...

We had twenty-four hours to leave; it was coming. All over the news, people were screaming, chaos was erupting, everyone in the continent was packing up and leaving as fast as they could, in any way they could. People were being trampled at the borders, fighting to get away. We left, running through forests and countryside to get away from the deafening screams of people being crushed. With ten minutes to spare, we were lost in a dense forest. It was coming, and we knew it would come for us first...

Rowena Jones (14)
The Purcell School, Bushey

We Have To Leave. Now.

The doors slammed shut, there was no escape. I pounded on the door, trying to get it to open, but it was no use. I was too weak and had not eaten for days. I tried running to the other side of the abandoned house but my feet felt like iron blocks being dragged along the worn wooden floor. My heart was racing, the sound of it thumping against my chest was deafening. I could not hear myself think. I took a long deep breath to calm myself down, knowing there was someone, or something, inside with me.

Madeline Hunt (15)
The Purcell School, Bushey

We Have To Leave. Now.

It feels like time has stopped. Our new lives are ahead of us. We committed a crime, that's why we're running. We didn't do it on purpose, it's not our fault that he tried to hurt me; it was only self-defence. I still sometimes see his cruel eyes losing life as the blade cut through his skin. His blood-curdling screams filling the halls of the mansion, but it had to be done. Now we have to start again. The dogs are barking, chasing us. Sad as it is, we have to leave...

Anastasia Valerie Helena Gould (14)
The Purcell School, Bushey

I Spy As Bullets Fly

Bang! Bang! Bullets flew by my head as I ran through yet another dark hallway, into a solitary hangar.

"I have to find him, he is humanity's only help!" I muttered.

"Where's he gone? Keep looking!" The guard's voice echoed through the hangar. As I crept along a long hallway, a guard shouted, "What are you doing? This area is off limits!"

Damn, I thought. I had to get through this door, to retrieve my enslaved wolf; he must smell the antidote for the chemical weapons The Organisation have been using on the world.

"Turn around now!" shouted the guard...

Michael John Lynch (14)
The Unicorn School, Abingdon

Monster!

Trapped within an endless abyss of agony. Encaged with a tormenting monster. I frantically ran, placing distance between us. Every day I suffer, there is no escape. Screams of sheer agony bounce off the walls, never stopping. My head slides off my sweaty hand, hitting my desk.
Bang! Throbbing, I lift my eyes, resting upon reality. On the board is the monster, staring into my soul. The teacher walked in slow motion, presenting a floppy white sheet. It is the monster I spent my life running from - there on my desk. I panicked, screaming with frustration.
"I hate maths!"

Millie-Maye Haggar-Rosewall (15)
The Unicorn School, Abingdon

Hunted

I had twenty-four hours to get the money to save my family, then my trousers vibrated. On the other end of the phone, a voice said,
"Eighteen hours left. In the background I could hear my family crying. I grasped my gun and went to the bank, stole £9 million, and narrowly escaped. I got £6000 for me, then I went to the abandoned coal mine. I heard my wife scream so I ran to the room where she was and gave the hunter the money.
"How much is there?"
"£8,994,000, and counting." He killed them and ran. I followed...

Will Fleming (15)
The Unicorn School, Abingdon

The Secret Purr

It's not safe now they know. All those years my secret had clung so perilously to my unnerving heart. But now the world knew! I had twenty-four hours to live, to die, to run. Tears executing my innocence, desperation seeped through my throbbing eyes as I clasped at anything that moved. "She has to be here!" I sobbed, collapsing to the ground. Reflecting across the forest, a glint of annihilation bounced off my cobalt eyes. As the inflicting allergies tore up my soul, a delicate purr haunted the forest. It had found me. Death had found me...

Florence Wallace (15)
The Unicorn School, Abingdon

Henry Edwards Is Hunted

My heart burned, freezing cold air sent chills down the back of my neck. The sinister sirens suddenly become louder. Rigorously I darted to get out of sight. Rattling gunfire. The ice on top of the lake cracked. I plummeted in... caught! Pitch-black. All I could hear was gunfire outside. Engine off, forced to the ground, guns jabbed in my face whilst my hands were handcuffed. Suddenly, my hands were free! I picked up an assault rifle. My head raced. Why did they pick me? I walked up to the hunters. They said, "Join us... be a hunter!"

Henry George Edwards (15)

The Unicorn School, Abingdon

Lost And Found

We landed at the airport, having lost our baggage. Seeing loads of armed police, we were worried we'd put something illegal in our baggage. I thought, what did I put in? It was filled with medicine and electronics, did they think we were trying to make a bomb for a terrorist attack during the flight? The police searched suspicious-looking people. They were asking if their baggage was on the carousel. We got angrier as were missing out on thousands of pounds. The police came to us and took us to a dark interview room... we got busted.

Adam Tate (14)

The Unicorn School, Abingdon

Last Breath

I couldn't run for much longer; I only had ten minutes before the ferry departed. Urgently, I limped along the fields with a sharp stick in my foot and bruises all over me. I did not look back. All I could hear were police sirens. I asked people for help, but they just ran away screaming. An unexpected flashing police car sped past but I just kept my head down. After excruciating miles of walking, I saw the ferry. I started to smile with relief and joy. But suddenly, I fell to the ground, bleeding, taking my last gasping breaths...

Ollie Mellor (13)
The Unicorn School, Abingdon

Suicidal Thoughts

The solitary siren wailed. The sky had grown darker again and the wind made queer sobbing sounds as it swept over the valley. Thunder growled. I saw a brief flash of lightning heading my way. Mist rising, my heart pounding. Running after her to tell her to stop, I stumbled over twisted roots that lined the unseen, uneven path, the howling wind roared against me, pushing me back. A police car raced by with its sirens screaming, heading towards where the girl was, at the edge of the cliff. Was she about to jump to her death?

Isabella Blase (14)
The Unicorn School, Abingdon

Trapped

You can't survive much longer. You turn your head, wondering whether it was still chasing. It was ten metres behind. Making a shrill buzzing noise, tearing through trees as if they were merely air! Your jacket catches on a thorn bush. You rip it off in urgent haste to be far away from the thing with the... eyes. Blood boils through your veins as if it too was trying to escape your hunter. Earth rises and falls under your feet. You burst through the trees onto a wide expanse of rock before a ravine. You are trapped...

Felix Iles Pounds (13)

The Unicorn School, Abingdon

The Hunted

We were so close. I looked behind me and saw flashing lights, and heard the deafening whining noise. I glanced over my shoulder and saw one of my men get viciously knocked to the floor by a massive alsatian. I thought to myself, all of this, just to keep a house. Suddenly, unexpected gunshots! I threw myself into a stream and lay for an hour under the bridge, feeling the ground shaking from the helicopters, I carried my bag filled with millions, and I saw the getaway car. I was never so happy to see a car in my life...

Freddie Cherry (13)
The Unicorn School, Abingdon

Chased

My heart was racing quickly, I was trapped, confused, and terrified. I was so scared that I felt like needles were being injected down my throat. Suddenly, I felt spiky painful claws scratching down my back, blood pouring as if it was a water fountain. I said to myself, I need to get out of here, but there was nowhere to go. I realised I was being hunted... I was running quickly to get to safety. *Bang!* I wondered what it was. I saw multiple entrances and saw freedom. I went with the darkest entrance...

Callum Byles (15)
The Unicorn School, Abingdon

A Force Of Nature

As I was running, the monster ripped through the house and sent it rocketing towards a field to the right. It whirled, shredding the road to tiny pieces. My legs froze in fear. But I had to run if I wanted to ever see my family again. The winds blew; the weather deteriorated as the rumbles and flashes scared me more. As I started to lose control of my legs, I got spun around like it was trying to break my body. Suddenly, the monster lost its grip. I flew far away and was forced into death...

Will Turner (13)

The Unicorn School, Abingdon

The Tournament

In the US, every four years they have a tournament. One person from each state gets picked and will fight to the death for their state. There are fifty states that go to fight each other. Finally, it is the day of the event. I pick speed and a gauntlet so when I see someone, I can click my fingers and they will die. We have twenty-four hours and then the shield will close in on you. Someone has a sword that can stop me clicking my fingers so I am unprotected. The games were about to start...

Jack Wright (14)
The Unicorn School, Abingdon